"**M**itch! Mitch, answer me! Get out of there, meet us at the ship bay! The aliens are loose! Spears is in the station! Mitch!"

An alien lurched out in to the hallway from an open door, turned towards the three of them, and opened those hellish jaws. Slime dripped from the teeth in long strings.

"Fuck you," Wilks said. He popped the carbine up, found the manual front sight – no time to mess with the laser – and fired a quick burst.

The armor-piercing rounds smashed the alien's face, shards of its hard chitin flew, acid sprayed. It fell sideways and backward, hit the wall, slid to the floor.

The blast of the caseless rounds hit Wilks's ears like a flat slap from a heavy hand. Should have put his plugs in. Oh well. If he lived long enough to worry about growing deaf in his old age, he could deal with that.

The liquid on the floor bubbled and sent up clouds of stinking smoke as it ate through the treadplate. "Watch the blood, don't step in it!"

They ran.

# ALIENS™

## BOOK TWO

# NIGHTMARE ASYLUM

## Steve Perry

(Based on the Twentieth Century Fox motion pictures, the designs of H. R. Giger, and the graphic novel by Mark Verheiden and Mark A. Nelson.)

### A DARK HORSE SCIENCE FICTION NOVEL

MILLENNIUM

First published in Great Britain in 1994 by
Millennium
The Orion Publishing Group
5 Upper St Martin's Lane
London WC2H 9EA

Millennium Paperback
Number Ten

ISBN: 1 85798 142 1

Printed in England by Clays Ltd, St Ives plc

For Dianne, of course;
And for John Locke, who probably would
have written it a bit differently . . .

Thanks go: to Mike Richardson, for the work and his input therein; to Janna Silverstein for her input and green pencil; to Vera Katz and Sam Adams for their oblique support. Couldn'ta dunnit withoutcha, folks.

"Now this is the Law of the Jungle—
as old and as true as the sky;
And the Wolf that shall keep it may prosper,
but the Wolf that shall break it must die."

Rudyard Kipling

# 1

Outside in the dead vacuum of space there was no sound; but inside the robot ship, the steady drone of the gravity drives vibrated like a low note played on some deep-throated musical instrument. It went through the flesh, to the bone; right to the soul; it had been there since the sleep chambers clamshelled up to expose their inhabitants to it. A mechanized *om* that lulled, as if calling them back into the long sleep, no chambers needed.

Billie sat in the makeshift kitchen, staring at what passed for coffee. The color was right, but that was about all. The taste was almost nothing, hot water with some vague taint to it. She watched it cool, stuck in the post-hypersleep lethargy, her own animation still feeling somewhat suspended. It was like the flu, you couldn't cure it and it just seemed to hang on forever sometimes. The coffee vibrated, making tiny ripples that lapped against the circular wall of the cup.

Behind her, Wilks said, "Tastes like shit, don't it?"

"That would be an improvement," Billie said. She didn't turn to look at him as he moved into the room. He sat on the bulkhead roll-out to her right and watched her for a few seconds before he spoke again.

"You okay?"

"Me? Yeah, I'm fine. Why shouldn't I be okay? I'm on a robot ship going God knows where, leaving behind an Earth overrun by alien monsters, in the company of half an android and a marine who is probably a borderline psycho."

"What do you mean 'borderline'?" he said. "Hey, I'm certifiable on any world you want to name."

Billie glanced at him. Couldn't stop the grin that matched his. Shook her head. "Jesus, Wilks."

"Hey, cheer up, kid. It's not as if things are really bad. We got each other. You, me, and Bueller." There was silence for a moment. Then: "I'm gonna go monitor the 'casts. You want to come along?"

Billie shifted on the crate she was using for a chair. Looked at Wilks. The burn scar on his face was something she almost never noticed anymore, but in this light, it gave his features a kind of wry malevolence. Like some minor demon out to play practical jokes. "No," she finally said.

"Suit yourself." He stood.

Billie sipped at the tepid liquid. Made a face at the nontaste. "Wait. I changed my mind. I'll go along."

It wasn't as if there was an awful lot to do on this tub. Since they'd awakened, a week had gone past, with no sign of stopping. Their monitoring gear was crappy, but even so, if there were any human-inhabited places around, they should have spotted them. The gravity drive was a lot faster than the old reaction sprayers, but if there was a planetary system, Wilks couldn't find it. There were better ways to die than starving on a ship going nowhere.

She should go and see if Mitch wanted to come with them. *Mitch*. She had trouble with that even now. Yeah, she loved him, but what a can of worms that turned out to be. Maybe not worms exactly, but whatever plumbing androids had installed sure looked verminlike. She loved him, but she also hated him. How was that possible, to have two such opposing feelings at once for someone? Maybe the medics in the hospital where she'd spent all those years were right. Maybe she *was* crazy.

The ship was fairly large, most of it was given over to cargo. They hadn't really gotten around to exploring all the nooks in it yet. Billie supposed that if they were stuck in it much longer, she'd get around to serious poking about, but the urge hadn't really come upon her; she wasn't quite bored enough. Why bother? Who gave a shit?

The control room was tiny, barely space for two to wedge their way into it. The designers had only to leave enough room for a repair tech, since the thing had been built to be run by the computer and a few service robots. The 'cast screens were blank, save for the two running ship data in computer language.

"Showtime," Wilks said. He wasn't smiling.

A man who looked like Albert Einstein at sixty said, "Have we got it? Have we got the uplink—okay, okay, listen, anybody out there, this is Hermann Koch in Charlotte; we're out of food, we're almost out of water, we're overrun! The damned things are killing or kidnapping everybody! There are only twenty of us left alive—!"

The man went away and abruptly there was another place. Outside, a bright and sunny day, spring flowers in bloom, bright green leaves sprouting on the trees. Only something hideous wrecked the scene:

One of the aliens carried under its arm a woman, as a man might carry a small dog. The alien was three meters tall, light gleaming from its black exoskeleton; its head was shaped like a mutated banana; it looked like some obscene crossbreed between an insect and a lizard. Boney, notched spars protruded from the thing's back like exposed ribs, three paired sets. It walked upright on two legs, a fact that seemed impossible given the way it was constructed, and a long, vertebrae-flanged, and pointed tail swept the pavement behind it as it moved.

A bullet spanged off the thing's head, doing no more damage to the hard surface than a rubber ball bouncing on a plastecrete sidewalk. The alien turned and looked at the unseen shooters.

"Aim for the woman!" somebody screamed. "Shoot Janna!"

Before the alien kidnapper could flee with its prey, three more shots boomed. One of them missed completely. One of them hit the alien's chest, flattened on the natural armor, did no harm. The third bullet hit the woman, just above the left eye.

"Thank God!" the unseen speaker said.

The alien sensed something wrong. It lifted the woman up, held her at arm's length, turned its head from side to side, as if examining her. The thing looked at the shooters. It dropped the dead or dying woman onto the sidewalk as if she were yesterday's garbage. Began to run directly toward the shooters. Made a hissing, burbling sound as it came—

Here, what was once a school classroom: but the rows of blank computer terminals were powerless; the only light was that which slanted in through a broken window. A human body lay on the floor, parts of it gone, eaten away, leaving a fly-blown swollen mass. Maggots squirmed in the rank remains, and the putrefaction had drawn ants and other small scavengers. The corpse was too far gone to say what sex it had been. Above the body, spray-painted on the wall in letters half a meter high the words: DARWIN ESTIS KORECTO.

Darwin was right.

Had the dead person written those words as a final statement? Or had the human arrived later, to contemplate them, to seek after truth—before the higher link in the food chain came for its due? Words like these had power, but in the jungle, the sword, the tooth, the claw, were mightier than the pen. Always . . .

A young man, maybe twenty-five, sat in a church, in the front pew. Religion hadn't been doing so well on Earth in the last twenty years, but there were still places of worship. A soft glow from beneath a cross mounted behind the altar illuminated the young man, who sat in the first row of the otherwise empty church with his eyes closed, praying aloud.

". . . And lead us not into temptation, but deliver us from evil," he said. "For Thine is the kingdom, and the power, and the glory, for ever. Amen."

Almost without pause, the young man began the prayer again, speaking in a monotone. "Our Father which art in heaven, Hallowed be thy name . . ."

A dim fuzzy shadow loomed suddenly on the wall at the end of the pew.

". . . Thy kingdom come. Thy will be done . . ."

The shadow grew larger.

". . . in Earth, as it is in heaven . . ."

There came a faint rasping on the floor, and if the young man praying heard it, he made no sign.

". . . Give us this day our daily bread. And forgive us our debts, as we forgive our debtors . . ."

The alien rose from behind the praying man, clear slime dripping in jellylike strings from its jaws. The lips cleared the sharp teeth. Its mouth opened, revealing an inner set of smaller teeth, more like a claw in their function.

". . . And lead us not into temptation, but deliver us from evil . . ."

The inner set of teeth was mounted on a greasy

ridged pole. The rod shot from the thing's mouth with incredible speed and power. The sharp teeth punched a hole in the top of the praying man's skull as if it were no thicker or harder than wet paper. Blood and brain tissue splashed. The praying man's eyes snapped open in a final surprise and he managed one word: "God!"

The alien caught his shoulders with its taloned hands and lifted him clear of the pew, the claws piercing flesh and drawing gouts of blood from a heart that didn't know it was dead yet.

The alien and its prey disappeared from view, leaving only a small puddle of congealing blood and a few flecks of gray matter on the pew to show they had been there.

The pew stood empty and silent.

God, it seemed, wasn't taking deliver-us-from-evil petitions just now.

Wilks leaned back and stared at the empty church on the screen. "Automatic camera," he said. "Probably set to catch thieves. Wonder how the signal got this far?"

Next to him, Billie's face was streaked with fresh tears. "Jesus, Wilks."

"Amazing how people keep sending the 'casts out. Like they really expect help. Or maybe it's like an old grave headstone, you know? The signals will go into space forever. Immortality as a radio wave. Maybe they think a million light-years from Earth somebody will pick them up and give a shit. You know, buy a bag of popcorn and watch the end of man, maybe on a double bill with a nature special."

Billie stood. "I'm going to see Mitch," she said.

"Give him my love," Wilks said.

She tightened, he could see her go tense, and he thought about softening it, but said nothing as she left. Fuck it. It didn't matter.

Wilks scanned the 'casts, looking for something different, but found only more of the same. Death. Destruction. Bodies rotting in the streets, animals feeding on them. A pack of dogs worried over a human arm. There wasn't any sound, probably a traffic cam, but he could tell they were growling and snarling at each other. The arm was bloated and slug-belly white. Been out in the sun too long, Wilks figured. Well. Whoever had owned it probably didn't have any use for it, might as well let the dogs eat it. It was just carrion now.

He shut the feed from Earth off. It was all history now. Whatever he was looking at had happened already, was over with, done.

He played with the scanners again, looking for wherever this ship might be bound. It was a crappy situation, the ship having been designed without passengers in mind. He'd managed to rig a few programs to get a read on the screens, which were only there for emergency backup anyhow, way he figured it. Probably cobbled together after things went bad on Earth, and as such was built with fence wire and prayer. After seeing the guy in the church, Wilks didn't have a lot of faith in prayer. Not that he'd ever had much to begin with.

The ship knew where it was going, maybe, but that didn't help Wilks. There must be a planet or wheelworld out here somewhere; there was a G-class star less than two hundred million klicks away, but if it had satellites, he hadn't spotted them yet. Had to be there, otherwise why would the sleep chambers let them out?

*Could be a malfunction, asshole,* the little voice in his head said with a smirk. *Could be you're all gonna die.*

Fuck you, Wilks told the voice. I got business to finish before I die.

*And you think the universe cares about your business?*

Fuck you, pal. You and the id you rode in on.

The voice rewarded him with a nasty laugh.

# 2

itch rested in the cradle they had improvised for him, and from behind it appeared that he was sitting up. Given that there was nothing left of his body from the waist down, sitting wasn't exactly possible. He stopped in the middle, almost literally half a man—half an android—a ragged medifoam blob sealing his innards shut. He had done the repairs on his circulatory tubules himself, shunting, reconnecting, so that he was once again a closed system. That was how he'd put it, a closed system. The other half of him had been left on the aliens' homeworld, torn off by a maddened drone protecting its nest. That alien was killed and likely it and most of the others there were vaporized by the subsequent atomic explosions Wilks had left them as a going away gift.

A man torn asunder as Mitch had been would

have died on that hellish planet, from blood loss or maybe shock. Androids were built better.

He heard her come in. This was the starboard computer access compartment, smaller even than the place where she'd just left Wilks. He heard her, but pretended he had not.

"Mitch?"

He shook his head. "I can't get past the operating system," he said. "Navigation access code is sixty-five digits, backed up by a second code of forty numbers. It would take forever to get it, given the hardware I've got. And where are the other ships? We left Earth in the middle of an armada. They should be somewhere around here, but they aren't. We're alone. It doesn't make any sense."

She moved to stand next to his cradle. Resisted the impulse to stroke his hair. "It's all right—"

"No, it *isn't* all right! We don't know where we are, where we're going, if we'll get there alive! I have to, it's my function to . . ." he trailed off. Shook his head again.

Billie wanted to cry, something she'd done more of in the last week than ever in her life. His *function*. She'd fallen in love with an android. Worse, maybe, he'd fallen in love with her. He was having more trouble dealing with the feelings than she was. When they'd gone into the sleep chambers, she'd accepted it, believed it would be all right, somehow. But when they'd come out, something had changed. Some of it was him. Some of it, she had to admit, was her.

She didn't think she was one of those people who carried her prejudices around like a club, bashing those who disagreed with her. She'd always paid lip

service to equality. A person is a person, no matter
if they're born of woman, incubated in an artificial
womb, or made in the android vats. Where you
came from wasn't important, only where you were
going. Spend too much time looking back, you'd
run into something and brain yourself, right? She'd
always said that. Androids were people.

Yeah, but would you want your sister to marry
one?

Or would you want to marry one yourself?

Jesus.

He hadn't told her, that was his main crime.
She'd only found out after they had become lov-
ers, after she had let him into her heart. That hurt.
She hadn't thought she could ever get past that,
but amazingly, she had. Or so she had thought. But
now?

It wasn't just that he was less than he had been.
With the proper facilities, Mitch could be made
whole again. As good as new. Meticulously designed muscles, perfect skin, all the right equipment in the right places . . .

Stop it!

No, there was something else going on here and
Billie didn't know exactly what. The man—artificial
or not—she had fallen in love with wasn't the same
as he had been. Something inside his mind was
different. She wanted to understand, wanted to
give him all the slack he needed, but he had become someone else, a cold, fearful person who
wouldn't let her in. Somebody who didn't want to
hear about her love or anger or needs. Hiding behind his wall, hands over his ears.

Still, she kept trying.

"Mitch, listen. I—" Now she did reach out and touch his hair. It felt as real as her own, was real in that it had grown from his scalp the same way, was made of protein so similar only a microscope could see the differences.

"Don't, Billie," he said.

She felt the words like a blast of frigid air, so cold it took her breath away. How could he do this? Not talk to her?

"Billie, please. Try to understand. I—I'm not trying to hurt you. It's—it's just that I don't—I can't—I . . . I'm sorry."

"I'm tired," Billie said. "I'm going to try to get some rest now."

She walked away, nearly tripped as the faux grav fluctuated a hair. They'd had problems with that, nobody thought a robot ship really needed gravity in transit and that system, like many of the others, had been rigged by Wilks before they lifted. To hear him tell it, if somebody sneezed too hard, the ship would break up.

The storeroom she used as her sleeping quarters was private, a three-meter-by-two-meter box, but since it was next to the ship's internal power and heating system, it was also hotter than most spots onboard. She stripped to her undershirt and panties, lay down, and leaned back against the bulkhead that served as a pillow. Sweat slid down her bare skin, dampened her clothes, and made her feel sticky. Still, it wasn't unbearable. And it was damnsure better than the company she'd have to endure otherwise.

She was dozing when Wilks appeared in the doorway. She hadn't bothered to slid shut the hanging curtain she'd rigged. His sudden presence startled her.

"Make some noise when you move, Wilks. You scared me."

He stepped into the room, his feet nearly touching hers. She sat up, drew her feet in. He'd seen her naked, but something about the way he stood there made her nervous.

"Everything scares you, Billie," he said.

She blinked sweat away, wiped at her eyes. "What are you talking about?"

He moved closer. Knelt. Reached out and caught her shoulders. "When you were a kid you were scared of dying. Later, you were scared of living."

"Jesus, Wilks, back off—"

He slid his hands under her shirt before she could react. Cupped her breasts. "And you've always been scared of me," he said.

Her shock turned to anger. She grabbed his hands, pulled them from under her shirt. "Goddammit! What the hell do you think you're doing!"

He grabbed her wrists, leaned against her. His face was only centimeters from hers now. She could smell his sweat, his . . . musk.

"You really prefer that *thing* in the computer room? Wouldn't you rather be with a real man? One who has all the right equipment?"

She felt something hard poke into her belly. Christ, was he going to rape her? "Wilks! Stop it! Why are you doing this?"

He jerked back, his face gone slack for a beat, eyes closed. The lids snapped up and an infernal light shined from his pupils at her. He grinned.

"Why? Because I'm going to make you face yourself. What you're afraid of. Love. Passion. Caring. People."

Billie looked down, and saw that the bulge she'd felt wasn't what she'd thought. It was his belly—

"Aagghh!"

With his scream, his abdomen burst outward in a spray of flesh and gore and a full-size adult alien came forth. Impossible, it wasn't physically possible! It smiled at her, showing the sharp carnivore's teeth. Slime and blood dripped as it reached for her . . .

"Wilks!"

Billie sat up, alone in her cubicle. Her shirt and panties were soaked with sweat, her hair hung limp.

Oh, fuck. A dream. Only a dream!

But she knew better. It wasn't a dream. It was a vision. A . . . communication. It was too real, it went too deep.

They were here.

On the ship.

Billie grabbed her clothes and ran.

Wilks was fiddling with the program that ran the external pickups, hoping to figure a way to magnify images visually when Billie rushed in. She was half into her coverall, drenched in sour sweat. There wasn't much water on this tub, they probably all smelled a little overripe. Even Bueller, who had sweat glands that did a fair imitation of human ones. He was in the other seat, having hand-walked in earlier, dragging his little plastic cradle behind him like some beggar from the streets of West L.A.

"Wilks, they're here. On the ship!"

She grabbed at his shirt. "Take it easy, take it easy! You saw one?"

"She dreamed about it," Bueller said quietly.

Billie turned and glared at him, as if he had violated some secret between them.

"It wasn't just a nightmare, Wilks. I *felt* them. Remember the spacefarer alien who saved us, how I could feel his hatred?"

"Yeah, the elephant man. Scavenger of doomed races."

"It was like that. I can still feel them. It's like some kind of light touch against my mind. I can't quite put my finger on it, but it is there!"

Wilks shook his head. The kid was stretched too tight. They all were, cooped up on this bucket. They'd been through a lot. The stress had to come out somewhere. He'd been doing sets of push-ups and chin-ups and squats every day until he couldn't move anymore, trying to burn it out of himself.

"Look, Billie, it doesn't make sense—"

"Where is the gun, Wilks? If you won't help me find them, I'll do it myself!"

Wilks looked at Bueller. The android looked away. Dealing with emotional women was out of his territory, Wilks knew that. Like it was something he knew how to do. Christ, women were like another species sometimes. He didn't understand them at all.

"Well?"

"All right. You want to play marine? We'll play

marine. But I'll keep the gun. We've only got part of one magazine left."

He stood, moved to the locker where he'd stored the carbine. He'd locked it securely away, along with the pistol he'd had before they went into the sleep chambers. He should have collected more ammo, maybe another couple of M-41Es before they lifted from Earth, a good marine armed himself as best he could when he could, but time had been a little tight. When your choice was hurrying to catch a ship leaving or staying to face either an atomic fireball or a hungry monster, you didn't dick around looking for spare ammo. He did have a couple of grenades for the under-the-barrel launcher of the carbine but those weren't much use on a vessel cruising through hard vacuum. Bust a hole in an external wall and the cold emptiness outside would suck your air out and freeze it into nice little crystals for you. Only a madman wanted to make something go *boom!* on a spaceship. Even the AP rounds from the 10mm could be a problem, but at least the hole they might make would be real small. Toss a Gum-sparrow into the stream and it would plug the leak okay.

He pulled the locker open, reached in, removed the carbine. Toggled the battery-saver off and saw the LED light. Five rounds left in the magazine. Shit.

Wait a second here, Wilks. It's not as if we're gonna need even five rounds. The kid is just tense. We do a run-through and show her we're alone and that's it.

He turned to Billie. "You want to take the handgun? It won't do shit to the armor, but maybe if it opens its mouth . . ."

"Give it to me," she said.

Wilks tendered the pistol, a slicked-up version of the standard army-issue Smith auto. He'd taken it from the general back on Earth, after the bastard had shot Blake. The general had gotten off three rounds, then Wilks had shot five more times. Eight. This model didn't have a counter, fucking regular army was too cheap to install them, but it was a fifteen-round double-stack mag, so it had seven shots left, eight if the general had kept an extra one in the chamber.

"Got seven rounds," he said.

She checked the gun. "I only need two," she said. Then she glanced over at Bueller. "Three."

"Okay, let's go find the monsters," Wilks said. "Bueller, you want to tag along?"

"Do you really think there is any danger?"

Wilks looked at Billie, then back at Bueller. "Truth? No."

"Then I'll stay here and continue to work on the computer."

Wilks could almost see Billie's anger smoldering. If he had said he thought there were aliens on the ship, then Bueller would have had to go along, being an android. To try to protect the two real humans.

"Let's move out, Billie."

Her jaw muscles danced and she nodded. "Fine."

What the hell, Wilks thought, it was something to do. So far, it had turned up exactly what he thought it would, zero. They'd been through all the ship big enough to hide a small dog and so far hadn't seen even an insect. Sometimes you got a few bugs on a ship, despite the zap fields supposed to keep 'em off. Some guys made pets out of them.

"That's it, Billie. End of sweep. Nobody home."

"What about the aft cargo storage?"

Wilks leaned the carbine against the wall and scratched a sweaty itch on his shoulder. "Can't get into it. Coded lock. We can't get in, nothing can get out, either."

"Come on, Wilks. I've seen these things operate. So have you."

"We could take a look at the door, that'll make you happy."

"It won't make me happy, but we have to check."

He shrugged. He could cut her a little slack. She hadn't exactly had a great life. Both parents killed by the aliens or, worse, webbed into hatching chambers as baby alien food. Years in a mental hospital on Earth where they thought she was nuts because the mind-wipe they'd tried broke down and let her remember it. And all the shit they'd been through since. What the hell.

The corridor leading to the aft cargo hatch was narrow and dimly lit. But Wilks could see down its length that the hatch door was shut and the LED on steady red-lock. Like all inner doors, it was airtight and proof against sudden decompression or hammering of fists—if somebody got on the wrong side of it during emergency. Standard duralloy plate, six or seven centimeters thick. Even the aliens could have trouble clawing through that.

"Knock, knock," Wilks said, "anybody home?"

The pair of them stood in front of the hatch for a moment. "Sorry, Billie. Looks like the hunt is over."

"What's that smell?" she asked.

Wilks sniffed. Something burned. It smelled acrid, like . . . cable insulation. A short somewhere? Could be easy enough, given how this ship was put together.

"It's stronger over here," she said, pointing toward the side corridor they'd just passed.

"Better check it out—"

A lazy wisp of smoke crawled from the corridor, a heavy vaporous snake that stayed low, hugging the deck.

"Better grab an extinguisher," Wilks said.

Billie pulled one of the portables from the wall.

Suddenly there came a loud metallic scream, the blare of a Klaxon. Foam from a ceiling fire suppressor sprayed into the corridor ahead of them, gushing from the cross-corridor.

"Shit!" Wilks said.

In his cradle Bueller saw the FIRE alarm visual flash onto the screen in front of him. "Shit!" There wasn't a PA system onboard. He couldn't call Billie and Wilks.

Using his hands, he flipped himself out of the cradle, hit the deck on his palms, and began to "walk" as fast as he could. It was awkward, but quick, as a man might move if he were late for an appointment but didn't want to embarrass himself by running.

•    •    •

The foam shut off and the Klaxon followed it a second later. Wilks sighed. That meant the fire was out. Or else the suppression system had given up the ghost. But he didn't feel any heat pour out of the corridor.

"Stay here, I'll check it."

"Fuck that. I'll be right on your ass."

He had to grin. "Okay. Watch it, deck's slippery."

They were walking parallel to the aft cargo compartment, and it only took a couple of meters to find the source of the smoke. A dangling cable, burned through, still smoking a little even though covered with fire foam.

"Wilks."

He turned to see what Billie wanted. There was a hole in the wall between the corridor and the aft cargo hold. A ragged, melted gap big enough for a man to walk through without touching the edges.

Melted by acid.

"Oh, shit," Wilks said.

Billie nodded. "Yeah."

# 3

Billie let the fire extinguisher drop as she hauled the handgun from her pocket. She clutched the pistol in hands gone sweaty and cold. Fear turned her bowels into a gelid lump. She wanted to run and hide, but there was nowhere to go.

"You were right," Wilks said. "I stand corrected."

He catfooted his way through the hole in the bulkhead, being careful to avoid touching the edges. "Careful," he said.

Billie followed him. The room was dark, a faint gleam from the corridor on the remnants of the fire foam the only light. No, wait, there were instrument diodes . . .

Wilks found a lume control and dialed the lights up.

"Jesus."

Billie nodded, her mouth too dry to speak.

Lying on the floor was an alien. Part of the deck beneath it was eaten away by its blood, a fluid so acidic as to defy belief. One theory Billie had heard in the 'casts was that it made the things taste bad. That was fairly horrifying. What kind of creature could possibly eat these monsters?

Along with the dead alien, the main cargo in the hold seemed to be four hypersleep chambers. Each had once contained a person. What was left of the four bodies wouldn't add up to one full-size corpse. The lids of the chambers were cracked and blood-spattered, human blood from the look of it, and long dried.

Billie felt like vomiting. She fought for control, won, but barely.

Wilks examined one of the control panels next to a ruined chamber. He turned back to Billie, who was glancing quickly around, expecting an attack at any second.

"These four were deep into it," he said. "Iced as cool as you can get without killing them. I think maybe somebody knew they were infected. Trying to keep the things growing inside the humans dormant. Looks like it didn't work."

"Why? Why would somebody do that?"

Wilks shook his head. "Dunno." He looked around, the carbine held ready. "Politics. Profit. We can talk philosophy later. Way I figure it, there were four aliens. Three of them killed the fourth and used its acid blood to eat themselves an exit. They've finished off breakfast"—he waved the carbine at the mostly eaten bodies—"and they'll be out looking for dinner."

"Mitch!"

"Don't worry about Bueller, they don't much like the flavor of android. We figured that out on the trip to their homeworld."

"But if they find him, they'll kill him."

"Yeah. Him and us, too. They must have left just before we got here. The acid triggered the fire foam. Come on. We need to get back to a section of the ship we can fortify."

Something rattled behind them in a dark recess of the cargo hold.

"Wilks—"

"I heard it."

He turned, brought the carbine up, flicked on the sighting laser. The tiny red dot danced in the shadowy corner.

Something hissed.

"Billie—"

The thing stepped out into the light. Three meters tall, gleaming black. If the monster had eyes, they were hidden from view as always, but whatever senses it used, it knew they were there. The external jaws opened and drool dripped from the rows of finger-thick needles that were its teeth. The spiky tail lashed back and forth like that of a cat about to pounce.

"Wilks!"

"I got it." He raised the carbine to his shoulder slowly. Billie saw the laser's red spot move up the creature's chest, over its chin, to shine on a lower tooth.

The thing's mouth opened wider. The red dot disappeared.

"Adios, motherfucker," Wilks said.

The *boom!* of the carbine was loud in the cargo hold, a blast that bounced from the hard walls and hurt Billie's ears. The alien fell backward, Billie saw the top of its head ten centimeters behind the jaws burst outward, tiny chips of armor flying as the bullet tore through. A thin stream of yellowish liquid spewed, painted the floor. It seemed to fall in slow motion, collapsing into a heap onto a hatch set flush into the deck.

"You got it!"

The hatch began to smoke where the stream of acid landed. More liquid pooled from the punctured skull.

"Out, Billie, out! That's a dump hatch, it leads to a lock between here and the hull! If that shit eats through the outer door—"

Billie didn't need to be told. She jumped for the alien-created door in the bulkhead behind her. Wilks was right on her heels. "Move, move!"

The fire alarm went off again, the hooter filled the corridor with noise. Foam sprayed inside the cargo hold behind them as they slipped and slid along the corridor still wet with the dregs of the earlier foam.

"Go, go, we've got to clear the next hatch!"

Billie was two meters ahead of Wilks when another alarm, more strident, began to blare. That would be the hull breach warning. The floor-to-ceiling hatch five meters ahead began to slide down, a light next to it lit and flashed red. Unless something plugged the hole in the hull, all the air on this side of the hatch was going to piss itself into the vacuum. Anybody on this side of the hatch was going to die trying to breathe nothingness.

Billie dived at the closing hatch, made it through, hit the deck. She skidded on her belly, felt the skin on her arms and hands scrape and abrade, but she was through! She rolled over. Saw that Wilks wouldn't make it.

He tried. He dived, stretched out full length, slid. But the door came down across the small of his back. Billie saw it press into his flesh.

"Aaggh!"

"Fuck!" Billie scrabbled on her hands and knees. She had to get something under the plate! A fire extinguisher, something! But there was no time, the door would break Wilks's spine in another second—

The gun. Billie still held the pistol. She shoved it, twisted it. Almost, not quite—"Breathe out!" she yelled.

Wilks couldn't see what she was doing, but he obeyed. She shoved as hard as she could and the barrel of the weapon touched the underside of the descending plate. When Wilks exhaled, it bought her a half centimeter. The back of the pistol's receiver skidded on the deck, got almost directly under the door, then stopped. The heavy plastic and steel of the gun creaked, began to bend.

Billie slid back, grabbed Wilks's wrists, and pulled.

"Come on, Wilks! Pull!"

The thin fabric of his pants snagged on the door, tore. The underside of the door scraped skin from his buttocks away, dug into the muscle, but he moved.

The pistol made a sound like a nail being pulled from wet wood as Wilks's thighs cleared the portal.

Billie shoved her heels hard against the deck, leaned back, and Wilks crawled up her, grabbed her shoulders, and pulled himself into a frantic hug, his feet sliding under the narrowing gap just as the pistol bent and shattered like a crystallized steel spring. Something sharp hit Billie's face just under her left eye. The descending hatch slammed into the deck as she fell backward with Wilks sprawled full-length on top of her.

Billie felt the muscles in Wilks's upper back relax under her hands. They lay pressed together for another second. Then Wilks drew a ragged breath and rolled off her to lie on his back next to her. After a moment he said, "Thanks."

Billie fought to slow her breathing. "No problem. I don't usually go this far on a first date, though."

Wilks shook his head. Managed a weak grin.


When the hull breach alarm went off, Bueller was halfway to the aft cargo bay. He had gotten fairly efficient at walking on his hands, but the sound made him hurry even more. Billie and Wilks were in danger. He had to save them. Especially Billie.


Wilks saw Bueller padding toward them, a distorted version of a man gone from the waist down. From the angle, it looked like somebody wading through the deck.

"Billie! Wilks!"

"We're okay," Wilks said. "Just another wonderful day on the exotic starliner cruise vacation. Come on." He extended a hand.

Bueller leaned to one side, resting all his weight

on his left palm. He reached up with his right arm. The two locked into a wrist grip, and Wilks pulled Bueller up onto his back. Bueller said, "Billie . . . ?"

"We've got company," she said. "Maybe next time you two will listen to me when I tell you something."

Back in the computer access room, Wilks began playing with the internal video cams. They weren't much, basic and cheap bottom-of-the-line Cambodian units. Terran regulations required such equipment, even on robot ships, and for once, Wilks was glad to see union politics doing something useful. No motion sensors or infrared, but something was better than nothing.

Bueller sat cradled in the operations chair. His reflexes were faster and he knew the systems better.

"We figure there are two of them left," Billie said. She leaned against the back of Wilks's chair, watching the monitors as Wilks brought up the various views.

Nothing in the main corridor.

"How did they get on board?"

Wilks said, "Somebody had four demi-stiffs in chambers in the aft cargo hold. Infected."

The midline cargo bay was clear.

"Why would anybody do that?"

"Good question. Fuck if I know." He winced. "Ah, shit."

"You okay?" Billie asked.

"Muscle spasm in my back. I'm not going to be running the marathon for a few days." He looked at Bueller. "Billie hadn't stopped it, the pressure hatch would have made me into your twin brother."

No monsters in the makeshift head.

Wilks brought up another view, this time of the kitchen they'd rigged. Nobody home.

"That's it," Wilks said. "Cheap bastards put in the minimum required, we're blind everywhere else. Damn."

Nobody said anything for a few seconds. Then: "I can maybe give us some more eyes," Bueller said.

Wilks turned. Pain shot down his spine, hurt all the way to his goddamn feet. He bit his lip. "What are you talking about? You aren't going anywhere."

"No, that wouldn't be very efficient in my present condition. But there are a couple of mobile cleaners, battery-operated dumbots. If we can rig a cam to one, we can program it to do a search."

Wilks managed a smile. "That's good, Bueller. And here I thought your brains were in your ass. Let's do it."


It took a couple of hours for Mitch to wire the things, but when he was done, they had a portable camera. Billie didn't know what they could do about it if they found the aliens, but she figured it was better to know where they were. They still had four shots left in the carbine.

The dumbot and camera were together as big as a medium-size dog. The unit rolled on six fat little silicone wheels and should be able to go anywhere a person could walk.

"Okay, puppy," Wilks said, "go find us the nasty monsters."

• • •

It took them nearly two hours to spot the aliens. They were on the ceiling of the corridor just outside the midline cargo section. If Wilks hadn't known they could do that, latch themselves to the ceiling, he wouldn't have had the camera doing full pans, but he'd seen the things come off the walls and ceilings of their nests. They weren't moving and if he hadn't known better, they looked like some kind of sculpture hung by a modern artist.

"There they are," Wilks said.

Billie leaned forward for a better look. "Now what?"

"I'm open to suggestions."

"I could take the carbine," Mitch began. "If I can get close enough before they move—"

"No," Billie said. "Can you make the robot make noise?"

Wilks and Mitch looked at her.

"Put it into the midline lock," she said. "If we can lure them into the lock . . ."

"Yeah," Wilks said. "We could blow them out into vac. Maybe."

"Better ideas?" Billie said.

Wilks and Mitch looked at each other. Shook their heads.

"Let's do it."

Bueller was good at taking over the dumbot with the remote. He got it through the inner hatch to the lock and started running it into the walls. They didn't have a sound pickup, but it must be thumping pretty good.

"Move it next to the outer hatch," Billie suggested.

Bueller did so. He trained the cam on the inner portal. Less than a minute later, the two aliens moved into view.

"Let's give them something to chase," Wilks said.

The dumbot moved back and forth in front of the outer hatch, Bueller had it going in jerky stops and starts.

"They probably know they can't eat it," Wilks said. '

"They're both inside," Billie said.

"Shut the fucking hatch," Wilks said.

Bueller abandoned the controls to the dumbot and slapped the override button for the hatch. Before the aliens could react, he grabbed the controls to the mobile unit again and sent it at the aliens. The little machine crashed into one of the aliens' legs.

The picture canted wildly as the alien kicked the robot.

"Grab hold of something, I'm shutting the gravity off!"

Wilks felt that familiar pit-of-the-stomach lurch as his body told his brain he was falling and would soon be smashed flat.

"Blow the outer hatch!"

Bueller hit the control. The ship wobbled.

"Can we get the camera?" Billie asked.

Bueller's hands did their dance, fingers wiggling impossibly fast. The picture spun. "It's outside the ship," he said. "Tumbling—there, there's one of them!" He froze the picture. One of the aliens floated past, its horrible expression made more so by the realization it was leaving the only sanctuary for millions of klicks. Or maybe that was just Wilks's imagination. .

"Where is the other one?"

"I don't see it," Bueller said. "But I've got a shot of the inside of the lock." He pulled up another image.

The lock was empty.

"All *right*!" Wilks said. "*Hasta la vista*, fuckheads!" He turned to look at Billie. "Score another one for the good guys, kid."

Her hair floated up around her head in the zero gee. She closed her eyes and nodded.

Bueller turned the gravity back on and Billie settled into herself—

Then something started banging on the hull.

# 4

The pounding that vibrated through the ship changed to a scraping noise. Like giant claws scratching on metal.

"Sounds like the cat wants in," Wilks says. "I'll get it."

He tried to stand. An invisible karate expert slammed a steely fist into Wilks's lower back. The spasm and pain nailed him into stillness. Any movement was too much. He collapsed back into the chair, and that hurt, too.

"Or maybe not," he managed through tight lips. "He probably hasn't had time to pee yet and we don't have a litter box."

"I'll go," Bueller said.

"Wait a second," Billie said. "Why does anybody have to do anything? It's outside. It doesn't have any air, it will freeze, it will die!"

Wilks shook his head. Damned if that didn't hurt, too. "It's not human, Billie. We don't know what kind of oxygen or energy reserves it has tucked away. It might survive a long time. Any of us would already be history out there."

"So? Fuck it, let it croak slowly."

Bueller picked it up. "This isn't a combat ship, Billie. No armor. There are things it could damage out there. Heat tiles and hydraulic sheathing will protect against atmospheric burns and space dust, but not against what that creature can do."

"What are you saying?"

"It jabs a finger in the wrong spot, bends the wrong flange crooked, rips the wrong hose, it might wreck the ship," Wilks added.

"I don't believe it."

"Trust me here, kid. A human in a suit with a half-kilogram reactionless hammer could do it. If it knew where to hit us, that thing could blow us to eternity and it wouldn't even work up a sweat."

Billie shook her head. "Great. Just fucking great."

"We have a couple of inspection suits," Bueller said. "Umbilicals. I'll see if I can rig one to fit me."

Billie stared at him. She took a deep breath.

Wilks saw it coming.

"No," she said. "I'll go."

"Billie—" Bueller began.

"A spacesuit has magnetic boots," she said. She stared at Bueller. "Is that right?"

"Yes, but—"

"So how are you going to move around and carry a carbine, Mitch? Hold the gun in your teeth while you clump around with boots on your hands? Wilks can't, you aren't in any shape to do it. That leaves me."

Wilks and Bueller exchanged looks. "She's right," Wilks said. "I hate that, but she's right."

Billie stripped to her undershirt and panties. The lock was chilly, the suit stiff and bulky as she stepped into the bottom half and worked it up her legs. Chill bumps frosted her skin; her belly felt as if it had been flash frozen from the inside out. Wilks had drilled her half a dozen times in how to put the suit on, how to test the seals, make sure everything was in working order. If he could have moved, he would have been here checking it. Of course, if he could have moved, he would have gone himself.

The suit had a voxcom; Wilks's voice came over it as Billie lowered the hard plastic helmet into place.

"Listen, kid, we can't be of much help in here. The internal cameras would freeze outside and this piece of shit isn't equipped with hull scanners. I might be able to rotate one of the long-distance sensors, but even so, it'd be fairly myopic."

"You want to watch it eat me?"

Mitch came on the com. "Billie . . ."

"Just a joke, Mitch. Don't worry. I'll find the damned thing and shoot it. I've got four shots left, that should be plenty."

She wished she felt as brave as she tried to sound. The odds were in her favor. She knew what she was dealing with, she had a gun that could kill it, she was brighter. The drones were like big ants or bees, they were nasty and deadly, but stupid.

That's what everybody said. Relentless, yes; smart, no. Faux grav was confined to the inside surfaces of the ship. Outside, the thing would float away if it wasn't very careful. Billie could walk on the hull with her boots; the alien would have to have something to hold on to. And it wasn't going to be her.

"Okay, I'm in the suit. The air is coming through, the heaters and valves and all are green, according to the little panel under my chin. I'm going to close the inner hatch and depressurize the lock."

"You sure?" Wilks said.

"Yes, Mother."

"Billie. Be careful." That from Mitch.

She could hear the love in his voice. She thought. She nodded, realized he couldn't see it. "Don't worry. I'm going to be *real* careful."

The pumps cycled online. The heavy suit expanded as the pressure dropped in the lock. God, she felt as if she were in a thick balloon. She could bend her arms and legs, but it was not easy. The carbine had been built with combat gauntlets in mind so she could reach the trigger okay in the suit's gloves. She made sure the fire selector was in single-shot mode. The LED number 4 on the magazine readout gleamed redly at her. Four shots should be enough. Should be plenty.

Another red light went on, this one a bar showing the lock's air pressure was effectively zero. Billie swallowed, her throat dry. "I'm going to open the outer door," she said.

"Copy. Go."

The hatch slid up. The stars were hard pinpricks against the dead black curtain of space. The local sun was shining, but on the opposite side of the ship. Billie moved to the entrance. Leaned out and looked to the sides. The ship had running lights and the faint glow was enough for her to see the immediate area was clear. A faint dusting of dreg-air blew out, becoming visible as it froze.

"Nobody in sight. I'm going out."

"Don't forget, your boot controls are on your hips, they're toggles. Put one foot out and light the magnetics on that side first."

"I remember."

Billie put her right foot outside the ship, lifted the protective cover over the button on her hip, pressed the control. The boot stuck to the ship's side without sound.

"The magnets are stronger under the arch of your foot, weaker at the ball and heel," Wilks said. "Walk as normally as you can and the boot will peel up and replant okay. It'll feel like you're stepping on something real sticky. Just take it slow, keep one foot down at all times."

"Wilks, you already said that. It wasn't that long ago; my brain hasn't gone dead yet."

Billie moved her other leg outside of the ship, triggered the magnetics on the left boot. Felt a sudden dizziness as she stood "up," extending from the side of the ship like a thorn stuck into it. She attached the magnetic ball of the umbilical to the ship as a backup.

"You'll probably feel like you're falling," Wilks said. "That's okay, don't let that bother you, you'll adjust in a little while."

Billie looked around. God, it was so *big*! Despite the fear she felt, a sense of wonder flowed into her. There was a kind of razor-edge beauty to it. The suit's heaters were on, she was comfortable enough, but the cold was so deep she could almost hear it sing. She sighed. It was a rush, being out here in the middle of nowhere, millions of klicks away from anything. It made her realize how small she really was, compared to the vastness of the cosmos.

"It's a real E-ticket ride out here."

"Ain't it, though," Wilks said. "You never forget your first EVA."

"Assuming you survive it," Billie said.

Walking was, as Wilks said, not too hard. A little awkward, but not bad once you got used to it. There was a little light on top of her helmet, and she switched it on. She felt as if she were the only person in the entire universe.

Wake up, Billie, she told herself. Don't forget why you're out here.

"I'm by the big dish-shaped thing," she said.

"The main antenna," Wilks said. "See anything?"

"Nope. I'm going to walk toward the back of the ship. I'll stay near the right edge so I can look down the side."

"Copy."

Billie started moving. She held the carbine ready to fire, her finger on the trigger. You weren't supposed to do that, you weren't supposed to touch the trigger until you were ready to fire the weapon, but she wasn't going to risk fumbling in the damned gloves when she couldn't feel anything through them. She'd heard the scientists were working on nanopuke suits that were thinner than paint and stronger than spider silk, you could see right through them, but the alien infestation no doubt put a stop to that fast enough.

She passed the parabolic dish, a couple of meters away on her left, glanced over to make sure nothing was crouched down behind it. The umbilical ball rolled soundlessly along behind her. She started to turn back and peer over the side of the ship when she caught a glimpse of movement in her peripheral vision.

Billie twisted back toward the dish, pivoting slowly on the balls of her feet. Her left boot peeled up from the deck.

The alien flew toward her like some malignant retro-bird, arms extended, taloned hands spread wide to catch her. It must have been flattened against the back of the dish, she thought. She should have looked higher. Bad mistake—

She screamed, something wordless and primal, and snapped the carbine up. Her vision tunneled, and she was vaguely aware of her yell echoing in the suit, of Wilks rattling something incomprehensible at her through the com. A single heartbeat later even those sounds vanished as all her attention focused on the black death sailing toward her. The distant sun glittered on the thing's armor, cast a long shadow over her, as it loomed, a living eclipse. Nothing existed for Billie in that moment save the thing's teeth, frozen spittle and slime crusting them as they came for her. She had the carbine up now, no time to aim, just point it and shoot—!

The recoil from the first shot peeled the other boot free of the ship. She couldn't tell if she hit the alien or not. The second shot's recoil spun her backward in a flip, her lower body and feet blocked her view of the onrushing monster. The umbilical created drag; the magnetic ball held. Instead of finishing the flip or sailing straight back, she arced downward toward the ship. Went over the side, still connected to the hull.

The alien flew at her, a meter away, but rising. One of her shots must have hit it, a stream of liquid sprayed from the top of its head, the fluid glittering and freezing into crystals as it spewed forth. The impact of the bullet had spun the monster slightly, but the spray of its blood coming out under pressure seemed to be pushing it back the other way. Toward her—

Billie fired the carbine again and again. She couldn't hear it, but she could feel the electronic click under her gloves as the weapon cycled empty. It was all so deathly silent—

Both rounds missed, as far as she could tell, but the recoil drove her away from the flying monster. It soared past her, missing by a good half meter. It did not go easily into the void. It twisted, tail lashing, inner jaws shooting out and snapping in what she thought must be rage. The thing turned slowly and continued onward into the vast emptiness.

Billie managed to tug on the umbilical and keep herself mostly facing the alien as it moved off. It was only when the thing was the size of an ant, a real ant, that she became aware of the com blasting at her again.

"Billie, goddammit, answer me!"

"Okay, okay. It's all right."

"What happened?"

"I found the cat," she said. "It didn't want to

come in after all. It wanted to go prowl the neighborhood."

"Buddha. And Jesus, too."

"It may run into Them where it's going."

"You okay?"

"Yeah."

"Come on in."

"Yeah. I hear that."

She hauled herself up the umbilical until she could stick her boots to the hull again. Oh, man.

As she was heading toward the hatch, she saw something glittering in the sunlight. The angle was just right, anywhere else she probably would have missed it. "Hello?"

"Billie?"

"Wilks, there's something floating next to the ship."

"The alien?"

"No, it's long gone. This looks like a contrail. Runs right toward the rear of the ship, but at an angle."

"Stray vapor, maybe," Wilks said. "From when we blew the aliens out. Or the dregs from your EVA lock-open."

"I don't think so. I can see some frozen air here and there. This looks like a jet trail. Real thin, but it seems to make a loop out in the distance. I can't tell at this angle."

"So it's an anomaly. Forget it. Come inside."

"I ought to go check it out, long as I'm here."

"I said forget it."

"Yeah, well, you say a lot of things, Wilks."

"Billie. Maybe it's alien piss. Or puke. It doesn't matter."

"Maybe. Maybe the other alien could pee hard enough to shove itself back to the ship."

"Come on. The things aren't that bright."

"You ever hear of anything that could survive hard vac without a suit? That could pound on a deep-space ship from the outside when it didn't have any air or protection from cold down around Absolute Fucking Zero? They might not be bright, but they die hard, Wilks."

The com was silent.

"I'll go see. Probably it's not anything."

"How many shots do you have left?" Bueller put in.

"Uh, actually, none."

"Dammit, Billie—"

"Doesn't matter," she said. "I don't have anything to shoot with, anyhow." The carbine was gone. She couldn't remember when she'd let it go.

"What are you gonna do if there is another one of those things there?" Wilks asked. "Insult its mother?"

"I'm just going to look. One thing at a time."

Bueller started to leave his cradle. "Where are you going?"

"Outside."

"Cancel that thought, mister. Not gonna happen."

"Sergeant, if there's another one of those things out there Billie won't have a chance against it unarmed."

"And you will? Last time you went up against these suckers you lost your ass, Bueller. And you are a bottle-bred marine and were armed."

"Wilks—"

"Civilization may be down the tubes but you're still a marine assigned to my command until you hear otherwise, ain't that right, Bueller?"

"You know it is."

"Then stay right where you are. We don't know anything is out there and therefore Billie is not in any clear danger."

Bueller bit down on his anger; Wilks could see him fight the desire to disobey the order. The programming won out. "All right."

"Good boy. Now, see if you can figure out something we can do if she gets to a place she does need help."

Billie walked down the rear of the ship until she was at the docking thruster. The gravity drives didn't use this thing; they were tuned to waves that ran completely through the ship, as she understood it, but for close order drill, the ship had rockets for maneuvers. As long as the gravity drives were operating the rockets wouldn't budge the vessel, that's what Wilks had told her.

The main thruster was a hollow tube a good three meters across, and it went far enough in so the other end of it was in complete blackness. The only way she was going to see that far was to lean over the rim and use her helmet light. Which meant that if anything was in there, it was going to see her when she peeped over the edge.

She told Wilks and Mitch what she was going to do.

Her breath was loud in the suit, the no-fog plastic of the helmet's faceplate was beaded with little drops of condensation, perfect, round spheres, unaffected by gravity, held together by surface tension.

"Okay. Here goes."

Billie pressed herself flat against the ship, using her hands to keep her steady, her boots touching only at the tips of the toes. She edged forward and leaned over the rim of the thruster, the lip of which was some slippery ceramic material. Managed to keep her grip as she was looking into the black hole.

Nothing. Least not from this angle. She edged farther out, to give herself a better view, all the way to the back of the thrust tube.

The little pool of light from the helmet splashed on the smaller reaction tubes that formed the rocket's spray controllers. Nothing. She started to relax.

Then she saw the alien. It was crouched against the reaction tubes, ready to spring. As if it had known she was coming.

"Oh, shit! It's in the thruster!"

Billie scrabbled backward, trying to get back over the rim. Her gloved hands slipped on the ceramic liner. Her right boot came free of the ship.

"Turn over!" she yelled at herself. "Get your fucking boots down!"

The monster raised its head and seemed to smile at her. It crouched lower. It was going to spring, and if she wasn't out of its way when it got here, it would catch her.

"Billie, get clear of the thruster!" Mitch yelled. "I'm going to fire it!"

"I'm trying!"

Time stretched, seconds became days, months,

eons. Billie twisted, tried to put her foot down, but had nothing to shove against. She pulled on the umbilical. It was loose, it didn't help.

"Billie!"

The alien sprang. It seemed all teeth and claws . . .

"Billie!"

In desperation, Billie realized she was trying to do the wrong thing. There wasn't any gravity out here. She didn't have to crawl backward on the ship, she just had to get out of the thing's way. She was thinking in two dimensions, but now she had wings. She shoved, as if she were doing a push-up. Flew away from the ship at a right angle—

"I'm clear!"

Fire blossomed, yellow-orange heat and light that nearly opaqued her faceplate as the polarizers turned the plastic dark against the wash of brightness.

She imagined she could hear the alien scream as it pinwheeled away from the ship, wrapped in a mantle of burning fluids, cooking within its shell. She took joy in watching it roast. Found herself grinning wolfishly. Yes. Fry, you son of a bitch, fry.

"Billie?"

"Nice shot, Mitch. Score another one for the good guys.

"*Now* I'm coming in."

# 5

Two days after Billie blasted the last alien into space Bueller picked up radio transmissions. The signals were on the military band and coded, so they didn't know what was being said, but from the strength, they had to be close. Unfortunately, the ship did not have any transmitters they could use, only receivers.

It didn't take Wilks long to figure out where the signals originated. "Hello," he said. "Lookie here."

Billie leaned over his shoulder as Wilks played with the computer screen. "Got us a planetoid. Not much bigger than a moon, but in direct orbit around the local primary. Been on the opposite side of the sun from us pretty much since we left the chambers, that's why we couldn't see it."

Numbers crawled up the screen. Wilks did something and the tiny blotch expanded and took on a roughly spherical shape, overlaid with grid lines.

"Colonial Marine base?" Bueller said.

"Yeah, that'd be my guess. Inflate a few pressure domes, pump 'em full of breathable, bury a couple gravity generators, and you got all the comforts of home. Provided you grew up in a barracks. Military has hundreds of these bases scattered around the galaxy. Or did have."

"Is that where we're going?" Billie asked.

"I don't see anywhere else, kid. If these crappy range finders can be believed, we'll be there in a couple more days."

The three of them stared at the computer-augmented image. Billie wondered if they were thinking the same thing she was: Was this a place of refuge? Or were they leaping from the frying pan into the fire?

It looked as if they were going to find out soon.

These damned gravity drives were something, Wilks had to admit. They were moving at speeds the old reaction ships couldn't touch. As they approached the planetoid—it was about the same size as Terra's moon—the constant drone of the engines shut down. The ship turned and began to retro, slowing their descent toward the only sizable chunk of real estate around for a hundred fifty million klicks. There was some rumble from the rockets, but compared to the thrum of the gravity drives, the ship was quiet. He had tuned the vibrations out, but now that they were still, he missed them.

"Might as well use what water we have left to

clean up," Wilks said. "We want to look good for the party."

"Yeah, especially since they aren't expecting company," Billie said.

He shrugged.

Despite his banter, Wilks was nervous. They were a long way from what any of them knew as home. Their reception was questionable.

The ship fell toward the tiny planet. The gravity increased as the military-industrial-strength generators on the base enveloped them in their fields. Bueller shut off the ship's faux gee and it got a little more comfortable.

The landing was rough; the ship fell straight in on its tail, the retros firing. Apparently it navigated some kind of gigantic hatched roof and wound up in a bay. The ship vibrated as compressors pumped air into the bay; when there was enough atmosphere, they could hear the machinery.

His back was still pretty tender, but Wilks could walk on his own. Bueller rode in his cradle strapped to a wheeled hand truck Billie had found. The aft cargo bay registered breathable air, and the three passengers made their way into it as the loading ramp was lowered from outside. The hydraulics whined as the back of the ship yawed wide and the ramp grated to a halt. It was cold, but the air felt fresher than what they'd been used to.

A quad of Colonial Marines in combat gear stood there, carbines held ready. At the sight of them, the four marines snapped their carbines up. Behind them, an officer sat in an electric cart, a fat cigar stuck in his mouth. He wore duty fatigues, and the gold braid on his visored cap identified him as a light general, a brigadier.

"At ease!" the general yelled. He stepped from the cart. He was medium height, but powerfully built, with the body of a weight lifter. He wore an opchan command headset, the bonephone and mouthpiece a single sculptured unit. He had an antique stainless 10mm auto pistol with full santoprene grips in a hip holster. The sleeves of his fatigues were rolled up to reveal several tattoos on his forearms: on the left, a rampant screaming eagle and chains; on the right, the Colonial Marine emblem and a dagger-and-banner. A rainbow holopatch shimmering on his left breast said T. Spears.

The general moved to stand in front of them. "I didn't expect to see you ambulatory," he said.

Wilks blinked. Nobody knew they were on the ship. If the general was expecting to see somebody *not* ambulatory, then he had to know about the human cargo.

"If you're talking about the four people in the freezers, that isn't us," Wilks said. "Sir."

The general raised one bushy eyebrow. "Say what, marine? Download it."

"We just came along for the ride," Wilks said.

The general nodded. "All right." To the marines standing by, he said, "Maxwell, Dowling, go check on the cargo."

"If you're talking about the four men in the sleep chambers, you're wasting your time," Billie said. "They were infected by aliens."

Billie wasn't slow. Wilks realized she also understood what the officer meant.

" 'Were' infected?"

"The aliens ate their way out. The men are
dead."

Wilks could see the general didn't care a lizard's
ass about the men. The general frowned. "What
about the aliens?"

Before Wilks could stop her, Billie said, "We
killed them."

The general's jaw muscles bunched. Wilks
thought he was going to bite his cigar in half.
"What? You killed my specimens?"

It was Billie's turn to blink. "*Your* specimens?"

"It was them or us," Bueller put in.

The general stared down at Bueller. "Listen, vat-
scat, I've got a base full of people, I don't need any
more. What I *needed* were those Terran-bred specimens! I *needed* to have my R&D people studying
possible mutations! There's a war on, mister, in
case you haven't heard. You just fouled up a Prior-
ity One mission. I could have you shot for that."

Wilks stared at the general.

He pulled the cigar from his mouth, tapped ash
from it. "Put these three in isomed and scan
them," he said. "Maybe they're infected and trying
to hide it. We might salvage something yet." He
tapped the command headset. "Powell! Get down
here, we got a snafu."

The barrel of the carbine jabbed Wilks in his tender back. He fought the urge to spin and smash the
marine who'd prodded him. He managed to keep a
grip on himself. No point in getting blasted by one

of his own after coming all this way. He'd go along. Maybe later he could figure out what the hell was what.

One of the marines pushed Bueller's carriage, the other kept his weapon trained on Billie and Wilks. Billie didn't understand what was going on. They went down a descending corridor. When they rounded the end, they were on the edge of a large room.

Billie gasped.

Against the far wall was a row of clear cylinders. The six tubes were four meters tall, perhaps two and a half meters in circumference. There was some kind of pale bluish, transparent liquid in the containers.

Each of the cylinders contained a full-size alien drone.

Billie found that she was digging her fingers into Wilks's arm.

"Jesus," Wilks said.

The marine with the carbine pointed at him said, "Not to worry, Sarge, those babies are in suspension. That's fluropolymer fluid. They're alive, but they ain't going nowhere."

Billie saw a dozen smaller containers lined up on a long table nearby. Each of those had one of the crablike alien hatchlings in it, ovipositors drooping limply under the fingerbonelike jointed legs. Several techs in osmotic clean suits stood or sat at the table. Billie, who had spent years in hospitals, recognized microscopes, surgical lasers, autoclaves, and other medical impedimenta.

Billie felt a wave of nausea. They were doing research on the aliens. Why? To learn how to kill them better?

That had to be it, didn't it? Why else would they be doing it?

# 6

The forklift rolled across the floor, thick slunglas tires silent on the smooth sheetcrete. The powerful electric motor hummed louder as the driver slid the special hoop clamps around the specimen container and lifted it. Carefully—the driver knew that breaking a container was a shooting offense—she backed off slightly, then pivoted the fork and headed for the queen's chamber.

Spears watched, nodding to himself as the specimen was carted away. The driver was good, she deftly avoided the hoses and power lines connected to the bases of the other containers in the vast storage room. Spears had more than a hundred of the alien drones undergoing suspension here, each of which had a complex chemical bath being pumped into it full-time. According the R&D scientists, the hypnotic chem flowing through the special drones should match their particular chemistry enough to affect them. To make them more amenable to outside suggestion.

Spears grinned, chewed on the end of his cigar. It was real tobacco, vat-grown and illegal as hell, but that didn't mean shit. Out here, he was the law. The cigar wasn't as good as those made from sun-raised and barn-dried leaf, but it was what he had. Oh, he still had six of the precious Jamaican Lonsdales left, *maduros* and dark as they came, each sealed in its glass tube of inert gas. But those were worth a fortune, he could get ten thousand credits apiece if he wanted to sell them.

He chuckled. As if money meant anything. Money was nothing, money was only a means to an end, the only reason you needed it at all was for supplies, equipment, to get things done. Here at Third Base, they didn't even use the stuff. The troops took what they were given and liked it or lumped it. The cigars had come from a vault in Cuba, a gift from a rich man who had been grateful to Spears for saving his ass in some dinky banana republic revolution. There had been eight of the valuable smokes. He'd smoked the first on the day he got his stars and command of Third Base. He'd smoked the second when his tame medicos had succeeded in bringing forth an alien queen and establishing her in a controlled hive. He planned to smoke the third after he won his first battle against the wild-strain aliens back on Earth.

Thomas A.W. Spears had plans, big plans, and they amounted to no less than the retaking of man's homeworld, using the deadliest soldiers a man had ever commanded.

He turned and strode toward his office, trailing smoke as he walked. A military man was bred for war, and in his case, it was truer than usual. He'd been among the first to be incubated in an artificial womb—he proudly kept the middle initials he'd been given at his decanting signifying just that—and it had been on a marine base where the first live births of AW children occurred. He'd been raişed in a creche with the other children, nine of them, and all but one had become Colonial Marines. The other one would have, if he hadn't been killed in an accident when he was still a prepube. Sure, the bulge-brains had come up with androids later, but he wasn't vat-scat, he was a real man, all his chromosomes in place, not a stray gene among 'em. A man who knew what he could do. What he *must* do.

The general paused next to one of the specimen containers. Put his hands on the thick Plexiglas. It was cold to the touch. The alien inside didn't move, but he imagined it could feel him, was aware of him, even in its suspended state. *Mark me,* Spears thought at it. *I'm your master. You live or die at my whim. Obey and live, disobey and die.*

He moved away from the container, took another look at the killing machine within. Hell of a soldier, this thing. Would destroy or die for its queen without hesitation. He nodded at the alien, then walked away.

He rounded the corridor's end and marched to the small office from where he ran the base. Damned civilian authorities on Earth had bollixed it up, just like they always did. Tried to fight a forest fire with little buckets of water, tried to extinguish a raging conflagration with spit and prayer. The only way to kill a big fire was to use a bigger blaze. Burn its fuel, choke its oxy off, eat what it would eat and starve it. Sure, you could punch holes in the aliens with armor-piercers, could blow 'em up with bombs, but that was wasteful. What better way to fight a beast than with another beast of equal ferocity? Something that could hunt the enemies down because it knew how they thought, because it was like them? Like a king snake will kill a poisonous viper or tame dogs will track a wild animal, the solution to the problem was painfully obvious. He hadn't believed that at first, until he got to know how the aliens operated. Now he was the strongest believer. The powers-that-were had been eliminated; now, it was up to him to carry on alone. No problem.

Spears reached his office, opened the old-style hinged door, stepped inside.

Major Powell, his first officer, stood next to the gunny running the computer terminal, peering down at the holoprojection that floated above the desk. Spears could read the words, even reversed and backward, if he wanted, but his first reaction was surprise and a little anger.

"Powell, I thought I told you to get to docking and clean up that snafu."

"Sir. It's as clean as it is going to get, sir."

"In my sanctum," Spears ordered.

The major nodded, said, "Continue, gunny," and preceded Spears into the inner office.

His office was spare, a chair, desk, comp terminal, couple of plaques on the sheet plastic walls. Spears circled the desk so that it was between him and Powell, but did not sit in the chair. "Well?"

"The ... specimen containers were ... destroyed, sir. Apparently the lowest survivable setting on the sleep chambers was insufficient to keep the specimens themselves dormant. The, ah, *containers* were dead, usual exit mode, to judge from the blood spray patterns, and mostly consumed. The adult-stage specimens apparently killed one of their own and utilized its blood to burn free of the area in which they were contained."

"Very resourceful," Spears said. He took his cigar from between his lips and looked at the cold ash on the end. He put the cigar down into the ashtray on his desk. "Continue."

"There were no signs of the other three—we assume all three survived—specimens. Acid burns in various places indicated a battle between the stowaways and the aliens. I have done a preliminary debriefing of the CM sergeant and from this report determined that one was killed by weapons fire onboard and the other two were ejected into space."

"Damn."

"Apparently the female stowaway went EVA and battled the remaining pair, who survived for some minutes in hard vacuum without apparent ill effect."

"The female did? Why not the marine?"

"He suffered an injury during the fight."

"Hmm. Well, the space stuff, we already knew they can do that. The in-head compression chamber and the—what's it called?"

"Pseudohypothalmic regulator," Powell answered.

"Right. Heats up the acid and keeps 'em from freezing."

"The corpses of the two killed on-ship were ejected."

"Too bad. We might have gotten something from the DNA." Spears looked at his dead cigar, thought about relighting it. "Two humans and half an android against four aliens in a close environment. I wouldn't have thought they could survive. Their tactics might be interesting."

"Apparently the stowaways have some prior experience with the aliens."

"Oh?"

"We don't have anything on the woman—the bounce from Earth is shut down—but the military bibliocom is bringing up records on the marine and android. The android, by the way, is Issue."

"One of ours?"

"Affirmative."

"Interesting. Are any of them infected?"

"Not according to the scan, no."

"Too bad. Let me see the squirt from bibliocom when it arrives."

"Gunny will have it in about eighteen minutes, sir."

"That's all, Powell."

"Sir."

Once Powell was gone, Spears sat. He leaned back, put his orthoplast boots up on the desk. Picked up the cigar and relit it. Took a deep drag and blew the smoke out in a blue-gray cloud. The ventilators whirred and sucked the smoke from the air. Maybe there was something to be gained here after all. It was a truly bad battle if nothing was gained; even the illest of winds sometimes blew a breeze or two of good. He'd see what the library had to say about this marine and android. And if they didn't have anything to offer, well, the techs could always use a couple more bodies in the hatching rooms . . .

"You okay?" Wilks asked Billie.

"Yeah, fine."

"You shouldn't have stomped on that guy's foot. He was just obeying orders."

"Yeah? So was the guy who nuked Canberra during the '82 Food Riots."

"How about you, Bueller?"

"No new damage," he said.

Wilks looked around. The room was bigger than some cells he'd been in. Five meters by five, fold-out bunks now flush against the wall, reinforced sheetplast, a double-thick door with a simple snap lock. A chemical toilet rested in one corner, bare white, no seat, a roll of wipes perched on a sink with a single water tap next to it. Nice place. A guy handy with a sliver of spring steel or stacked carb could pop the lock easy enough. Thing was, on a world where everybody lived inside a pressure dome, where were you gonna go even if you did get out? They might steal another ship, but without some knowledge of navigation, not to mention knowing which human settlements were still un-tainted by alien infection, they wouldn't have a clue about where to go.

"Did you see the monitors we passed?" Billie asked.

"Yeah. They've still got spysats in place, military view only. That major who stopped and questioned us? He told me they could keep tabs on the war. He seemed like an all right guy. Almost apologetic. We'll probably be hearing from him again."

"I don't have much experience with the military mind, Wilks. What is going on here?"

"Hell if I know. The general looks like a lot of RMs—that's regular marines—I've known. Eats, breathes, and shits the Corps. Probably runs the base so tight it hums. Probably doesn't matter to him that Earth is down the tubes, he's got his orders and that's what he lives by. Or else he's got delusions of godhood—lot of generals get that way—thinks he can do anything. Hard to say which it is."

"What do you think he's going to do with us?"

Wilks shook his head. "Dunno. He's obviously running some kind of experiment with the aliens. My bet's it's—or was, when still it mattered—very hush hush. Top-secret stuff. We're sand in this guy's well-lubed machine."

"You take me to the nicest places, Wilks."

He laughed. "Can't say it's been dull, can you?"

Billie managed a smile. "Nope. That's a word that never crossed my mind. So, what now?"

"Ball is in their court. We wait and see what they do with it. Get some sleep." With that, Wilks unfolded one of the cots and climbed onto it. Bueller did the same, pulling himself up easily and sprawling onto the thin material. After a moment, Billie pulled a third cot loose and lay on it.

Wilks had been in the military long enough so he could sleep pretty much whenever he wanted. Whatever was going to happen was going to happen. He'd deal with it when it got here. Within a few moments, he dropped off.

# 7

The three marines were in one of the third-level *inodoros*, crowded into the space designed for a single toilet and sink. The walls had eyes all over Third Base but they figured the crapper ought to be safe enough. The room was made yet tighter by the backpack one of the men had propped on the white plastic HWDS-C— human waste disposal system, chemical, in military parlance.

"How much did you get?" one of the marines asked. That was Renus, Wolfgang R., Private First Class.

"Three days, if we stretch it," the marine balancing the knapsack said. He was Peterson, Sean J., Corporal.

"Shit," the third marine said. "It's four days to

the civilian terraforming colony, five if we stick to the canyons." Magruder, Jason S., also PFC.

"So we'll be hungry when we get there," Peterson said. "Listen, I was pushing to get this many meals. Spears has everything on this fucking base inventoried, down to the paper clips. Besides, the crawler will have E-rations, carbocons."

"Great, if you like greasy sawdust," Magruder said.

"Hey, you can fuckin' stay here if you'd rather."

Magruder shook his head. "Like hell."

Renus said, "You think the civilians will take us in and keep quiet about it?"

Peterson shrugged. "They've dealt with Spears. They know he's over the edge. They'd be worried about him thinking they had a hand in helping us, if they did or not. My guess is, they'll hide us and tell him they never heard of us."

"Still risky," Magruder said.

"Like I said, you can stay here. Sooner or later you'll stumble over some reg you never heard of and you know what that means."

Magruder nodded. "Yeah. Baby food."

"How long you figure we got?" That from Renus.

"Couple–three hours, maybe," Peterson said. "Spears and Powell will play mad doctor with the stowaways. Our general likes to watch the implants, I think it gives him a hard-on when those things shove their eggs down somebody's throat. If we can get to the Thousand Canyons and the heat faults, they won't be able to see us on IR. The crawler's cammo should cover us from visual."

The three men looked at one another.

"At least it's a chance," Peterson said.

They filed out of the *inodoro* into the hallway.

At the South Lock, Patin, Robert T., PFC, was on security. He leaned against the wall, his carbine propped at an angle next to him. He looked up, saw somebody approaching. He smiled, but didn't bother to assume any kind of guard-ready position. Sloppy work, but he doubtless had the same attitude about lock-duty as most marines: You couldn't get in from outside unless you had the admit codes and if you did, you were okay; you could get out, but—who would want to? The planetoid wasn't what you'd call a pleasure dome, now was it?

"Hey, Renus. You come to keep me company?"

Renus drew near. "Take some more of your money playing cards, you mean? Nah, I wish. Decker sent me to relieve you. Circulating pumps on Four are showing red in the backup chamber. Guess who is the only qualified pump-tech on duty?"

"Fuck," Patin said. "Red means automatic suit-up. Why didn't somebody call when the cocksucker went yellow?"

"Don't ask me, Bobby. I don't run things around here."

Patin pushed away from the wall, stepped across the hallway toward the computer terminal inset into a panel at chest level. "I'll punch it into the security com and it'll be all yours, pal. Can't be too careful these days."

The guard couldn't see Renus pull what looked like a sock full of something heavy from under his shirt. "Sorry, Bobby," Renus said.

"Huh—?"

Renus slammed the sock down on Patin's head. It made a sound like a thick rope slapping a plastic barrel full of liquid soap. Tiny slivers of gray flew from the sock on impact. Lead shavings, sparkling like glitter under the overhead lights, drifted onto the unconscious man's downed form.

"Let's go!" Renus yelled.

Peterson and Magruder came running up. Each of them had a carbine. Renus grabbed Patin's weapon. They had the codes for the inner lock door and cycled it open quickly.

The outer door's codes were something else. While Peterson took a stab at the computer override, Magruder pulled climate suits from the racks. He and Renus shrugged their way into the suits.

"Not gonna happen," Peterson said. "Security seals are dogged down tight. We'll have to burn the sucker. I'm trashing the alarms."

Magruder, his helmet in place, the suit tabbed shut, nodded and moved to the door. He pulled the plasma cutter he'd stolen from Supply and thumbed the cutter up to full. "Watch your eyes," he said.

The brilliant plasma jet spewed, turning the inside of the lock into noon on a desert. Peterson kept his eyes covered until he got his climate suit on and the polarized faceplate snapped down.

It didn't take long. The security bars were designed to keep people outside from getting in, and the plasma jet ate through them almost as fast as Magruder could move the welder. Durasteel went bright orange, then flowed molten and fell in fat drops.

"That's it, that's the last one!"

"Go, go, go!"

The lock door started to open, then ground to a stop with a shriek still audible in the escaping air, stuck where a flange of partially melted metal caught the frame. But it was wide enough for the men to get through. They clambered from the station into the cold darkness, and ran toward the motor pool. The gravity generators extended the field outside the domes for a hundred meters around, so they didn't bound into space.

The trio of deserters piled into the first crawler they reached. After a moment the multiwheeled machine lurched into the darkness and was gone.

Spears leaned back in his chair, watching the video on his holoproj. "Replay, security cam 77, 0630 hours."

The air above his desk lit with the images of the three marines in the loo. "Increase volume one-eighth. Continuous tracking."

He watched it again, listened to the three marines plotting their desertion. When they left the toilet stall, another hidden cam just outside the *inodoro* picked them up without missing a beat.

The scene at the security station played itself. The downed guard didn't get any sympathy from Spears. If he'd been doing his job, he would have stopped the deserters. Well. There was a place for men like the guard. Down in the hatchery.

Spears watched with interest the burn-out through the lock door. They moved well as a team, the trio. Too bad they chose treason instead of duty.

"General?"

Spears glanced up from the projector to the door. "Come."

The door opened and Powell stood there. Spears waved one hand and shut the projection over his desk off. "Yes?"

"The squirt has arrived from bibliocom. In the system."

"Query number?"

Powell gave it to him.

Spears tapped it manually into his terminal. "What's the marine's name?"

"Wilks."

He tapped that in.

The air blossomed again with the infocrawl. Images fluttered into life to join the words and figures. A practiced speedreader, Spears scanned the material.

"Well, well. We sure this marine is the same one in isomed?"

"Got a positive ID from his magnetic femur implant. It's him."

"This sergeant has had more hands-on experience with wild-strain aliens than just about anybody except that civilian, whatshername."

"Ripley, sir."

"Right. Nobody knows where she is but we got Wilks right here. How's that for luck? Fate smiles on us, Powell."

"Sir. And if you'll scan the android's file, you'll see another coincidence, sir."

"Give me the gist."

"He was one of a Specials Unit, bred to travel to the aliens' homeworld. Under the command of Colonel Stephens, prior to Terran infestation."

"Stephens, I remember him from MILCOM HQ. A desk jockey, couldn't find his dick with both hands."

"The primary mission, retrieval of a specimen, was apparently a failure, sir. Records of the trip are incomplete; by the time the survivors reached Earth, the infestation was in the advanced stages."

"And the woman?"

"No records on her. She's not military, and we can't pull up any history." Powell shrugged. "You know how civilians are about record keeping in the best of times, sir."

Spears nodded absently. "Well, our sergeant and the vat-boy have got actual combat experience against the wild strain. Much too valuable to turn into incubators, at least until after we find out what we can from them."

"That's what I thought, sir."

"Let's go have a little talk with them."

"Sir."


Billie felt a coldness grip her legs, bands of rough steel encircling her ankles, pulling her knees apart. She blinked, glanced down, saw she was naked.

Something wet and slimy dripped onto her bare belly. A clear, ropy jelly. She looked up, but couldn't see the source, there was a kind of fog hovering over her, only centimeters from her face, a featureless gray.

*I need you,* came a deep voice. No, not a voice, the words were unspoken, they were in her mind. They were the thoughts of a lover, but not a human lover.

The fog swirled away, and teeth glittered under a

coat of clear slime, white needles set in a massive black jaw, on a long, impossibly long head that flared into wide, flat, branched antlers.

Billie gasped, fear filling her, every cell in her body straining to contain it.

*Lean back.*

Unable to resist the command, Billie arched her neck, saw just behind her a massive, fleshy egg, easily the size of a garbage can. Flaps at the top of the egg opened, spidery webbing stretching and breaking. It was like the blossoming of some obscene flower, petals spreading wide in a photographic time-lapse hurry.

Crablike legs reached over the folded flaps, long, fleshless finger bones with sharp tips, questing, exploring. Looking for something.

Looking for Billie.

She opened her mouth to scream, and a glob of the slime from the monster above her fell onto her chin, oozed into her mouth, over her cheeks, into her eyes. Billie tried to swallow, but it was too much.

*I need you.* The monster's thoughts tried to soothe. *Do not be afraid. It will be good.*

"No!"


Billie came up on the cot, yelling the word.

"Easy, easy," Wilks said. He was next to her, holding her shoulders. And on the floor, balanced on one hand, the other hand on her leg, Mitch.

Billie blew her breath out in a big sigh. Shook her head. There was no need to say it. Wilks knew. He dreamed, too.

She looked at Mitch. Did androids dream?

"Up and at 'em, people," came a voice from the entrance to the cell.

A pair of armed marines stood there.

"General wants to see you," one of them said.

"Tell him our calendar is full," Wilks said.

The marines grinned. The same one said, "Not me, Sarge. You tell him. Move out." He waved the carbine.

Wilks looked at Billie and Mitch, shrugged. "Well. Since you insist."

With Billie pushing Mitch on his cart, the three of them left the cell.

# 8

The table was, nearly as Wilks could tell, black glass. Expensive for an officers' mess on some back-rocket planetoid. Course, it could have been made from local mineral and not brought in on-ship; even so, it was not something you expected to see. The chairs were some kind of basic fold-out issue, but they'd been padded and spiffed up by somebody with skill and time.

Billie sat to his left, Bueller to his right, the three of them occupying one end of the table. Another dozen people could sit along the sides, but those chairs were empty. Spears sat at the other end, alone. A platter of what looked to be roast meat sat in front of him, aromatic vapors wafting from it. A long knife and double-tine fork were stuck in the meat.

"It's not real beef, of course," Spears said. He

pulled the knife and fork from the roast and ran the edge of the blade back and forth against the fork tines, as if sharpening the knife. "Protein hard-jell and soy, but our mess sergeant has a deft touch with seasonings. It's not bad."

With his hat off, Spears was as bald as an egg. Nothing but eyebrows and lashes, from what Wilks could see.

Spears stabbed the roast with the fork and began to slice the ersatz beef.

An orderly, dressed in kitchen whites, came from the doorway behind Spears. By the time the general had the first slab of roast carved free, the orderly arrived and shoved a plate under it. The timing was perfect. Half a second later and the "meat" would have flopped onto the black glass. Spears never looked to see if the plate was there.

The general repeated the carving. A second orderly scooted from the doorway and arrived in time to push another plate under the falling slice of roast.

The third slice, yet another orderly.

It was offhand, but every bit as impressive as a precision drill team tossing carbines back and forth at speed. Spears knew it, too.

When the plates had been delivered to Wilks, Billie, and Bueller, along with glasses of red liquid—wine?—and eating implements, the general carved himself a slice.

The fourth orderly was a bit slow. He thrust the plate out, caught half the roast. For a second, it looked as if the fake meat would flip from the plate and smack onto the table, but the orderly juggled his cargo and managed to slide the slab back into place. It left a smear of gravy on the white plastic, but stayed put.

Spears's jaw muscles tightened once, then his face relaxed into a somewhat forced smile. He nodded at the orderlies. "At ease, troopers."

The four orderlies filed out via the door by which they'd entered.

Wilks would not want to be the last one, the one who had nearly bobbled the general's own meal. He had very nearly made the general look bad. On a military base, that was as dangerous a crime as a soldier could commit.

The general raised his glass. "To the Corps," he said.

What the hell, Wilks thought. He lifted his own glass. Noticed that Billie and Bueller did the same, albeit without much enthusiasm.

The wine wasn't bad. Wilks had surely drunk a lot worse.

"Eat," the general said.

The cook was inspired, Wilks had to admit. The counterfeit beef was as good as any he'd ever had. Right texture, right flavor—if Spears hadn't told him, he wouldn't have known the difference. Not that he got a lot of real meat on the money he made anyhow. Rabbit now and then, fish, even chicken on special occasions, that was about it. Last time he'd had what was supposed to be certified beef had been at his old top kick's mustering-out party couple years back, bio-time. Given all the suspended animation travel since then, it was a lot longer in realtime.

Whatever was going on inside Billie's head,

Wilks could see she was enjoying her meal, too. As for Bueller, who knew? His model of android could eat, even cut in half as he was now; whether he enjoyed the food in the same way a basic-stock man did or not was something else.

"Food okay?" the general asked around a mouthful of it.

Wilks nodded. "Very good."

Billie and Bueller also nodded and mumbled something. This was strange territory and wherever this conversation was going, they'd decided to play along. For his part, Wilks was pretty sure this guy's wingnuts were dogged down too tight. It didn't make sense to set him off until they had some idea of what he was all about.

"You'll have to excuse my somewhat abrupt manner when we met," Spears said. "There's a war on, one can't be too cautious." He smiled.

Jesus, Wilks thought, it looks as if his face might crack from the strain. This cocker wanted something from them, that was plain enough. What?

"It has been brought to my attention that you have had considerable experience with wild-strain aliens, Sergeant Wilks."

Wilks chewed on the beef. Swallowed it. "Yessir."

Spears popped another chunk into his mouth and chewed it thoughtfully. "Been in combat against them in several theaters, correct?"

"That's right, General."

The man nodded. His eyes seemed to take on a brighter gleam. "Good, good." He looked at Bueller. "And you, Issue, your injury was sustained in combat as well, was it not?"

"Yes, sir."

"These men are military, marines, I know about them. What about you, little lady?"

Wilks saw that Billie couldn't bring herself to speak. "Sir," he put in, "Billie was on Rim during first contact with the aliens. The only survivor."

The general raised one of his thick eyebrows. "Is that so?"

Dumbly, Billie managed a nod.

"She survived on her own for more than a month," Wilks said.

The general's other eyebrow went up. "Really? Most resourceful. How old would you have been then?"

"Ten," Billie managed.

Another of the face-threatening smiles. "Excellent." He ate another bite of the meatless meat. "I envy you three, you know. You've been in combat against the toughest enemies, the most dedicated soldiers men have ever faced. Perfect troops, fearless, tough, almost unstoppable. Your survival is quite an achievement. A fluke, really, but no less heroic for that."

He pushed his plate away, less than half of the meal eaten. An orderly zipped from the doorway, removed the plate, refilled the general's wineglass, and vanished almost without a sound. Spears leaned back, sipped at the freshened wine. "The only way to beat an enemy as hard as the one man now faces is to use troops of equal vigor. Ones who can match the ferocity of the opposition."

That got through to Billie. "You're trying to raise tame aliens here?"

"With the proper leader, my troops could spearhead the retaking of Earth," Spears said. "Think about it. What better way? The wild strain behave like ants. With troops of equal caliber plus proper strategy and tactics, they wouldn't stand a chance."

Billie started to say something. Wilks kicked her under the table. She closed her mouth.

"Great idea, sir," Wilks said.

The general nodded, pleased. "I knew you would see it so," he said. "You've been up against them, you know how little chance humans or even specially bred androids have." He nodded at Bueller, gestured with his wineglass.

"How can we help, sir?" Wilks said.

Billie looked at him as if he had lost his sanity. He kicked her under the table again without changing his expression.

If Spears noticed Billie's look it didn't seem to register. "Your experience, Sergeant. I have computer-generated scenarios, recordings of battles on Earth, theories. You three have been there, you know the reality. I want your advice, your knowledge. My troops must be as well prepared as they can be when I formulate my strategy."

"Certainly, sir," Wilks said. Stretched his own scarred face into a smile. "Bueller and I are marines before anything else. And Billie wants to help, too, isn't that right, Billie?"

Billie nodded. "Right."

Spears was practically beaming now. He raised his wineglass. "A toast, then—"

But before the general could offer the toast, the major came in via the same door the orderlies had used.

Spears frowned. "What is it, Powell?"

"Sorry to disturb your meal, sir. A security breach. The guard on the South Lock has been assaulted, the outer door burned open. One of the land crawlers is missing."

The general waved one hand. "Oh, that."

Powell blinked. "Sir?"

"This is my base, Major. I try to keep up." He looked at Wilks. "You have to stay on top of things when you're the CO. Enjoy the rest of your meal. You are free to go anywhere on Third Base; you have full clearance. If you have any questions, Major Powell will be happy to answer them. I suppose I should go and see to the malcontents who have destroyed military property."

With that, he stood, gave Billie a military bow that was barely a nod, and left with Powell.

Wilks stared at the general's back as he left. Wished he had a gun at that moment.

In the hallway, Spears said to Powell, "Keep an eye on them. Put the android in rehab, see if we can give him mechanicals or whatever so he can be ambulatory."

"Sir."

"And that guard from South Lock, put him in the egg chamber. He fucked up."

Spears felt a happy satisfaction at watching Powell swallow dryly when he gave him that order. The universe had become a place where only the strong, the ruthless, could survive. Sentiment was for another time. In the past and, someday when he had won this war, in the future. Meanwhile,

somebody had to make the hard choices and
Spears was the man to make them.

Billie found she was shaking. She wasn't sure if it
was because she was afraid or angry. She stood, but
Wilks was right there. He hugged her, and before
she could do more than stiffen and start to pull
away, he whispered, "Play along, Billie. They probably have a cam on us and a voice recorder."

She relaxed a little. "What?"

"If we don't do what this guy says, he is going to
feed us to his monsters. Play along."

The thought of that turned her bowels to lumps
of dry ice. For a moment she couldn't even breathe.

A marine private entered the dining room and
started to wheel Mitch away. Billie turned quickly.
"What are you doing?"

"Major's order, ma'am. Taking the AP to Rehab."

"Why?"

"Don't ask me, I'm just doing what I'm told."

"It's okay, Billie," Mitch said. "It's like putting
your flitter into the shop for repairs."

Billie stared at him. The marine wheeled him
away.

"Relax," Wilks said, his voice at normal volume.
"The general just wants to make sure his troops are
cared for properly. I don't know what kind of facilities they have here, but my guess is they can fit
Bueller into some kind of lower body exoframe, at
least, so he can get around on his own."

Billie couldn't think of anything to say. This was
all so damned weird.

"Come on, let's explore a little. Might as well get

acquainted with our new home, eh?" He winked at her.

Billie nodded. She understood. The more they knew about this place, the better. "Yeah," she said. "Good idea."

# 9

Days passed; Wilks and Billie explored the base. It was like a dozen such places Wilks had been on in his career, standard hardware from the lowest bidder, as cheap as it could be and still work. The one thing he noticed that bothered him wasn't the gear, but the people. There didn't seem to be enough of them for a base this size. If anything, the military usually had too many troops for the work needed, a larger command being what officers liked to wave at each other. Warm bodies meant more than cold rock. Given the extent of the base, almost as big as a very small town, there ought to be several hundred more people staffing it.

Eventually, Wilks and Billie worked their way into places not so easy to find or reach.

"What's in there?" Wilks asked the guards posted in front of a large double door.

The two troopers, one male, one female, wore holstered sidearms but they didn't seem particularly worried that they would need them. The man, who looked to be almost two meters tall, smiled down on Wilks and Billie.

Wilks said, "The general has given us the run of the base. You want to open the door?"

Now the woman grinned. "You don't wanna go in there, Sarge. Show him, Atkins."

The tall man touched a control on the wall.

Billie gasped.

"Fuck," Wilks said.

"Hell, she don't even have to do that," the woman said. "She's fertile all by herself."

The projection floated in front of the wall. A queen alien occupied the center of a huge room, a monstrous sac jutting from her rear like some obscene, translucent intestine. The sack, webbed with supports that ran to the convoluted ceiling and walls, was obviously full of eggs, and as they watched, the queen deposited yet another onto the floor already thick with the things. A pair of attendant alien drones stood in a puddle of fluid near the sac's sphinctered opening, and they gently moved the fresh egg to one side as the queen began to lay another one.

"Still want me to open the door?"

"Why are you even guarding it?" Wilks managed.

"Pan right," the woman said.

The taller guard stroked a slide control. The holoproj shifted as the camera panned.

Webbed against a wall in front of a neat row of

eggs were ten humans. The cottony material holding them in place hid most of them, leaving only
the faces bare. Some of the people were awake,
eyes wide. Were they already infected, or still waiting for the horror yet to come?

"Turn it off," Billie said.

As Wilks and Billie walked away from the
stomach-turning scene, the tall marine, obviously
enjoying himself, said, "Have a nice day, folks."

They weren't there to keep anybody from getting
in.

They were there to keep anybody from getting
out.

Spears watched the image of Wilks and the
woman as they turned away from the projection
outside the egg chamber. They were weak, like
most people were weak. But he could use them.
That was the important thing.

He looked at his chronometer. "Ah, the mice are
about ready. Time for the cat to wake up and
move." He touched a control on his desk. "This is
Spears. I want First Platoon, A Company, saddled
up and ready to ride ASAP. Full combat gear, full
field rations. I'll be at the South Lock in ten minutes. Better not keep me waiting, marines."

Wilks went to shower, water being one of the few
things they had plenty of on the station. Piped up
from some deep underground cave as ice chunks
and melted on the way up by heaters in the slurry
conduits, SOP for this kind of operation. One of
the few perks even grunts got.

Alone, Billie wandered down narrow hallways,

feeling as if she were being watched. God, this was all so insane. Having spent years in a mental hospital because the authorities thought her memories were hallucinations, Billie had some experience with madness. This was right up there. Spears ought to be in a silicone room somewhere, doped to the hairline, scheduled for a full mental revision. Who were those people in there with the queen alien? What had they done to deserve such a fate? No crime could be so awful as to rate that kind of sentence. Spears was bug-fuck crazy and he should be put away. Instead, he commanded troops and had a personal nest full of the deadliest things man had ever encountered. What kind of deity would allow that kind of lunacy? Only one that was crazy itself.

She came to a door marked Communications. It slid open as she approached.

A tech sat, a comhelmet covering half her head, staring at a series of flat screen monitors. The tech looked over, saw Billie. "I heard we got visitors. Come on in, I got a notice says you're cleared for this area."

Billie stared at the woman. Why the hell not?

The door closed behind her.

Wilks sluiced the cleaner from his body, enjoying the feel of the hot water against his skin. They were in deep shit here, no doubt about it, but you had to take it as it came. He had expected to fertilize the flowers on the alien homeworld. Hell, he'd been living on borrowed time since the first time he'd run into these fuckers on Rim all those years ago. He should have died with his squad then, it was a miracle he hadn't. And the years of trying to hide from it and from the nightmares that wouldn't go away since hadn't been all that pleasant. He had been ready to pack it in, to take the Big Jump and the hell with it, but before that happened, he got pissed off. He'd blown the aliens' homeworld flat and that hadn't been enough. Somehow, for some reason, he was still alive. It didn't make any sense. He'd never been a religious man, but it was like he had some kind of higher purpose driving him. He'd been too lucky, as if somebody had looked out for him. He was tired, he wanted to tube the whole mess, but he couldn't. It was as if he had been given the responsibility to take care of this little problem—the extermination of all those monsters that had nearly wiped out humans.

It wasn't fair, nobody could expect one broken-down chem-head marine to do that, but while he couldn't pin it neatly to any logical wall, Wilks felt as if that was exactly what he was supposed to do: save mankind.

Damn. And he couldn't even float very well, must less *walk* on fucking water . . .

The old man was white-bearded, his left arm bandaged crudely from wrist to elbow, his clothes dirty and torn. A dark and grimy baseball cap was pulled down over his head and whatever hair he might have left. He had an antique rifle lying next to him, something that appeared to be blued steel and worn wood, an old-style bolt-action piece, probably a hunting weapon from a hundred years past. Back when people hunted for sport and not for survival. He sat cross-legged, leaning against a pile of rubble, mostly broken furniture and shattered building material; a small campfire burned in front of him, the flickers from it painting the old man's face yellow-orange.

A girl of about six leaned against the old man's side, her face dirty, long hair matted.

"Here comes Air Sammy," the old man said. He pulled a vial from his jacket pocket, sprinkled a powder from it into the campfire. The fire sputtered and the flames turned a bright blue-green. "I hope the bastards have their spookeyes on."

Overhead in the night, the running lights of military attack jets appeared, red and green against the smog that was mostly smoke. The rumble of their engines increased.

"Will they see us, Uncle?" the little girl asked.

"I hope so, honey. They should." He waved at the blue fire.

The fiery lance of a missile erupted from one jet, then other rockets followed. Like meteorites, the missiles streaked and died quickly, to be replaced by a brighter flash of light followed by artificial thunder as the rockets exploded.

"Stupid fucking airheads," the old man said.

The little girl covered her ears with her hands as more explosions rocked them. A blast wave streamed the little fire as might a man blowing gently on a candle.

A woman moved into the circle of firelight. She looked a worn fifty, her clothes were smudged with ashes and dirt, and she had an airpump shotgun on a sling over her shoulder. She squatted next to the little girl. "Hey, Amy. You okay?"

The little girl looked up. "I'm okay, Mom. Did you find anything to eat?"

"Not this time, honey. Maybe Leroy did. He should be back soon. Damn!"

This last followed a louder boom and brighter flash of light. Dust and small bits of debris swirled over the trio, and the fire flattened briefly under the blast.

"Why do they bother?" the woman asked. "They hardly ever kill any of them and the damned things just don't get scared."

"Fucking airheads," the man said. He glanced around. "We'd better move out, Mona. The things will probably start their sweep after Sammy shears off."

"What about Leroy?" the little girl asked.

"Don't worry about him, baby. He will meet us at the reservoir. He knows we can't stay here."

The old man looked across the fire, and spoke as if there were an unseen watcher sitting there. "That's it for now, sports fans. Tune in again tomorrow, same time, same satellite, for another exciting episode of *Life in the Ruins of Earth*. We'll sign on at 1900, if the bugs haven't eaten us. Summer's over and it'll be getting dark sooner. That's a dislink and endit—"

He pointed an old-style IR remote control at the unseen watcher and the three people vanished . . .

Billie gripped the arms of the plastic form-chair tightly and found she had been holding her breath as the image on the viewscreen went blank. She forced herself to relax. To breathe.

"They're regulars," the tech said. "Amy, Mona,

Uncle Burt. Sometimes Leroy—he's Chinese, we think. The kid looks to be about six. Our guess is that her mother is in her late twenties, some of the stuff she talks about. The old guy is maybe seventy, probably not related, though the kid calls him Uncle."

"God," Billie said.

"I don't know why they bother 'casting," the tech said. "It's not like anybody is going to drop down and help them."

Billie shook her head. "Maybe it's all they have left. It matters that they try. People do that."

The tech shrugged, scanning for another image. "Or *did* it. This base location is classified information," she said, "but I can tell you that the 'cast we just saw is history. Even in cold sleep and with full race gee drives going through the hypercut we are a long way from Earth. The little girl could be years older by now. That, or worm food. It's a message in a bottle."

Billie's insides clenched. She knew just how that little girl must feel.


Something about being clean and in fresh fatigues made a man feel better. When you faced death as often as Wilks had, minor shit like crazy generals didn't seem so bad. While he couldn't say he felt the same detachment about the Long Nap some of the Zen martial arts boys had, Wilks had looked Death square in the face enough times so it didn't scare him. You lived or you died, that was how it went, and when your number came due, you got collected. He'd thought his was at the top of the pile several times but Death had only grazed him when he reached for another. Fuck it. A hot shower and clean clothes, however, were tangible, something you could relate to in the here and now. The ground might open up and swallow you next step, a stray comet could zip in and squash you like a bug, one of the aliens could hop from behind a garbage can and eat your face off, but those were in the unseen future. Right *now*, Wilks felt pretty damned good. One second at a time.

Being cooped up on that drone ship hadn't given him any love for it, but Wilks found himself walking toward the vessel because he had an idea. The thing had been unloaded and it would need new fuel cells and probably some repair before it had any chance of being spaceworthy again. It sat in the middle of one of the big prefab storage areas, a mostly dark and very cold room that apparently wasn't worth spending more than the minimum on for light and heat.

Wilks's footsteps echoed hollowly as he walked across the sheetcrete flooring toward *The American*. The cargo bay door was still open, and the ship's internal lights were off. He walked up the expanded-metal incline and slapped the light button. It was a little warmer inside the ship, the fuel cells' heat sinks radiating their excess warmth into the air.

Wilks moved deeper into the cargo hold, found an empty hex storage crate, and sat on it. It was very quiet, only the low hum of power units audible. After a few seconds Wilks heard what he expected: boot steps outside the ship.

Whoever was following him was approaching.

Wilks flexed his hands, rolled his shoulders. Prepared himself to move, if he needed to move.

The footsteps drew nearer.

Billie worked her way toward the medical section. She wanted to see what they were doing to Mitch, if she could.

On the other side of a clear door inside a smallish chamber that looked like an anteroom combined with an airlock, there was a short, fat man dressed in a lab cloak and what looked like white paint. She touched the plastic wall and it was very cold. He spoke to her through an electronic passthrough. "This area is Clean," he said. "You want to come inside, you have to be deloused first."

Billie blinked. "Deloused?"

"Chem- and electro-instillation," he said. He waved at a horizonal cylinder about the size of a coffin on a metal frame against one wall. "All your internal and external flora and fauna get zapped. No stray bacteria allowed. Then you get spraysuited." He rubbed his leg with one all white hand. "Osmotic, lets your skin breathe air, keeps everything else in—including sweat."

That would explain why it was so cold in the room, maybe. "Seems like a lot of trouble."

"Regulation sterile technique. Can't have some wild micro-animal messing up experiment protocols. Even though the UV overheads usually catch any we miss, you never know. If you're just planning to satisfy idle curiosity, better you should look at it on the holoproj. That'll save you a lot of B-time."

"B-time," Billie said.

"As in 'bidet.' When all of your intestinal bacteria get fried, it tends to do interesting things to your bowels. After your first delouse treatment, you tend to get a real fulminant diarrhea that lasts about a week. Cuts down on your personal mobility, it does."

"Ah. I'm looking for the Artificial Person who came here with us."

"The 'droid? He's in mechlab. They're molding him for an exobase and walker. Won't take all that long. I can connect you on the com."

Billie thought about it for a moment. "No. That's okay. I'll talk to him later."

"No problem. You need anything, just ask. I do what I'm ordered, no mistakes."

As Billie wandered away, she thought about what the fat man meant by that last remark. It had been another long day. She was tired. All she wanted to do was lie down and sleep.

No, not sleep. Not with the aliens here to infect her unconscious mind and make it churn out nightmares.

She had thought the hospital awful. Had feared for what they planned to do to her mind, the chemical lobotomy the medics had decreed.

Given all that had gone on since she'd escaped, a mind-wipe didn't sound so bad.

# 10

Wilks saw the man step
into the cargo bay, but not who he was—the hangar
lights were dim and the ship's standby lamps were
not much brighter. The man looked around.

"Over here," Wilks said.

The man tensed, dropped his hand toward his
hip and the handgun clipped there, then froze. He
straightened, then moved closer.

"I thought it might be you," Wilks said.

It was Powell.

"What do you—?" Wilks began.

Powell gave him a cut wave. Wilks shut up.
Watched as the major pulled some kind of electronic sniffer from his belt and touched a control
on it. A green LED lit on the little black plastic
rectangle. "Okay, clear."

"Walls have ears?" Wilks said.

"And the ceiling has eyes. Everywhere on the base, except in here. Another few days and this ship will be bugged, too."

"Spears."

"He's as paranoid as they come. Crazy as a spider on a hot griddle, you know."

"Yeah, I figured."

"He lives for his scheme of retaking the Earth and being the hero of the millennium. He thinks everybody is out to get him. He runs a poison scan on his food and still makes an orderly taste it first; he sees conspiracies everywhere. In normal times the mindbenders would be lining up to write books about him."

"Normal times," Wilks said. "Been a while since then."

Powell nodded. "Yes." The man paused, sighed, seemed to gather his thoughts. "Maybe we're beyond reason as a species. Maybe what mankind needs is a sociopathic psychotic killer to match the aliens." He shook his head.

"But you don't believe it," Wilks said.

"No. It would be a step backward, a return to the caves. We're . . . better than that. We have achieved civilization, the stars. We can't go back."

"Not to defend Spears, but dialogue doesn't seem to work too well on these things."

"I understand that. But the queens are intelligent. They *can* be communicated with—we've done it here. Our queen is cooperating, after a fashion. They want what we want, to survive, to thrive."

"If you're preaching the 'Brotherhood of Life' line, Major, you're wasting your time. I've seen my friends slaughtered by these fuckers. I was on Earth just before they nuked a big chunk of it rather than get eaten alive."

"I know, I know. I'm not saying we should hug the aliens and expect smiles all around. Sharing the same world with the aliens isn't likely, they're too much like we were half a million years ago, too egocentric to think of life forms other than their own. No, I'm not suggesting any such thing. But we are supposed to be intelligent, to be civilized. War is stupid, annihilation of an entire species is barbaric."

"Funny, coming from a major in the Colonial Marines."

"Not all military men are killers, Sergeant. Neither are all officers automatically savage morons."

"Could have fooled me," Wilks said. But he grinned. Powell was somebody with a conscience, and he was obviously trying to do something here. Wilks wasn't sure just what, yet, but he had a feeling he was going to find out.

"They didn't nuke it, you know."

"What?"

"Earth. Didn't happen. No major atomics, nothing but tacticals, according to our feeds."

"Probably because your friendly neighborhood aliens ate the guy supposed to push the button."

Powell shrugged.

"Okay, so, what's the scat, Major? Why are you telling me all this and risking your own ass?"

Powell nodded, and took a deep breath.

The atmosphere plant was never going to produce a surface nitrogen-oxy mix thick enough so unaugmented humans could use it for breathing purposes, unless they crawled in the bottoms of deep craters. True, the planetoid was big enough to hold some gases down with its feeble gravity but the term "terraforming" was something less than exact in this case. Unless you thought of humans as moles or perhaps prairie dogs.

No, the civilian colony was here because there were a vast number of underground caverns that could be sealed tight, filled with air, and used either as shelter or to grow enough food to sustain a permanent population. Once the tiny world became self-supporting, there were plenty of uses for it: expanded military bases, mining, an escape-proof prison. It was to those ends the terraformers worked. What the atmosphere plant produced was, save for venting, pumped into the ground.

The stolen crawler approached the plant, slowed. Came to a stop. Inside the small craft the trio of deserters were four days from a bath and out of food.

"We made it," Renus said.

"Yeah, so far," Magruder added.

The crawler's pilot at the moment, Peterson, nibbled at his lip, but said nothing.

"Radio's still quiet, 'cept for stray stuff from Third Base," Renus said.

"Spears would have them on a war footing, no transmissions—like there's anybody out there who gives a roach's ass."

"Yeah," Peterson said, "but we ought to be picking up suitcoms or Doppler or something this close."

"This isn't a place where people go out for a picnic, now, is it, dickhead? They're all underground."

Peterson glared at Renus, looked as if he were going to come up from the seat and take a swing at him.

"Bury it," Magruder said. "We made it, that's the important thing. Spears didn't even come looking in this direction; we didn't see any flyovers. We're home free."

"I'll feel better when I'm inside," Peterson said. "Be a hell of a lot easier to steal a ride offworld here."

"So what are you waiting for?" Renus said. "Move in."

The crawler started forward.

In the hold of *The American*, Powell said, "He's been feeding the experimental subjects all kinds of chem the scientists say might have some effect on the things. We don't know if it's working or not. The body chemistry of these creatures is astounding."

Wilks touched the scar on his face without conscious thought. He realized what he was doing, dropped his hand, said, "Yeah. I noticed. Acid blood probably fucks up your basic tranquilizer pretty good."

"We've done some conditioning exercises with the queen. She doesn't appear particularly concerned with the fate of individual drones—we've killed them and she doesn't display distress in any way that shows. But if we threaten or destroy any of her eggs, she becomes very agitated."

"Fetch the stick or we squash the babies?"

"Something like that, yes. It seems to work. And the queen controls the drones—we aren't sure how, some kind of telepathic or extremely low frequency radiopathic waves, something. We—ah—we've put a single human subject into a chamber filled with alien drones, given him an egg and a blowtorch with which to threaten it, the queen watching, and none of the aliens touched the man."

"Jesus, you're cold-blooded fuckers."

"It wasn't my idea, Wilks. Spears runs the show here."

"Why doesn't somebody put a bullet into him? Shove a grenade under his bidet?"

"He has his supporters. And like I said, he's very careful."

Wilks shook his head. "He trust you?"

"Not really."

"But you could put him away. Then you'd be in command."

"I'm not a killer, I told you that."

"Yeah. Go on."

Powell went on.

Billie was in the room they'd issued her, a closet-sized cube big enough for a bed and chair, the sink, shower, and toilet all in a walk-in space inset in one wall. She'd just finished cleaning up. She didn't want to sleep, but she was so tired she knew it was going to happen soon. One of the medics she'd talked to had given her a tablet he said would help. She wasn't the only one on the base who had bad dreams, so it seemed.

She was staring at herself in the tiny mirror over

the sink, wondering who this thin, hollow-eyed woman was.

"Billie?"

She turned. Mitch.

They had repaired him, after a fashion. He was held in a bipedal frame by shoulder straps and a wide band across his chest and waist. The platform began where his body ended, and extended into a pair of hydraulic struts, pistons and stainless steel and stressed plastics that terminated in oval pads nothing like human feet. They hadn't tried very hard to match his proportions—he was about eighteen or twenty centimeters shorter than he'd been with his own body intact, so his hands dangled at the mechanical knees of the legs. Billie's flash image was of a man who had been stripped of flesh from the waist to his toes, then had his skeleton chrome-plated and hung with cables.

"So," he said. "Is it me, you think?"

The joke fell flat and it broke her heart that he tried it. But if that was how he wanted to play it, she would give it a shot.

"I think the flitter salesman sold you a demonstrator. You should have held out for next year's model."

The silence began, stretched too long. He broke it, finally. "They don't have an AP vat-works here, this is the best they can do." Another moment stretched, a spiderweb made of silken time hit by an insect in slow motion. "You okay?"

"Now that you ask, no. My homeworld is in ruins, my love life is for shit, I'm stuck on a military base with a guy who thinks he can keep monsters in a kennel like pets. The galaxy is going to hell in a hearse, Mitch, or hadn't you noticed?"

She turned away, so she wouldn't have to look at him.

"Billie, I'm sorry."

"Why? None of it is your fault, except the love life part. In the grand cosmic scheme of things, that doesn't count for a whole lot anyhow. Forget it."

"Billie . . ."

"What, Mitch?" She spun around and glared at him. "What are you going to *do* about it? Did the technicians hide a nice little expandable dick in that thing?" She pointed at the exoframe. "Pump it up and it stays hard all night?"

He blinked. Raised one hand, started some gesture, then dropped it. Shook his head. Turned and walked away. The quiet whine of the hydraulics grew quieter, the thumps of the pseudopods faded away.

Billie sighed and it turned into a sob. Oh, man. She'd stepped over the line. Leapt over it like she was wearing rockets. She'd wanted to hurt him and she had. They apparently didn't teach him how to fight when it came to emotional stuff and she fought dirty, going for the throat. Oh, man. How could she do that?

*How,* came the little voice from deep within her mind, *how could he make love to you, make you fall in love with him and not tell you he was an android?*

Was there any doubt about whose sin was the greater one here?

Billie took the tablet the medic had given her,

swallowed it dry, and fell on the bed. Pulled the flat and hard pillow over her head. Life was so unfair.

What an original thought that was.

With the crawler docked, the three marines exited and found themselves in the antechamber of the air plant. The locks were coded but some helpful civilian had scribbled the admit number over the pad.

"Christo, what a bunch of fuck-offs," Renus said.

"It's not like they're gonna get a lot of company out here, now is it?" Magruder said as he punched in the code.

The inner lock slid open and the three padded inside. Once the door sealed behind them, they removed their helmets.

"They might not take too well to visitors waving guns," Peterson said.

"Yeah, well, until we know which way the hydrogen fuses, I'll feel a lot better holding on to mine." He waved his carbine. An armed marine should be worth thirty unarmed civilian air farmers.

"If they give us any flak, we go to plan B—the shuttle," Magruder said.

"Will that thing really get us anywhere else?"

"It got the farmers here, didn't it?"

"Yeah, but who'll fly it? Not you." That from Renus.

"Whoever flew it here," Magruder said. "We'll make him a reasonable offer." He patted his own carbine.

Peterson snickered.

The corridor was wide, dark, with high ceilings. The lighting was bad.

"Spooky in here," Peterson said. "And hotter than the Devil's dick, too."

"Some side effect of the gas generators," Magruder said.

"Who made you an expert on this shit?" Renus said.

Their footsteps echoed as the trio walked down the corridor.

"Where the fuck is everybody?" Peterson said.

"Maybe they're having a party," Renus said. "An orgy. I sure could use a little pussy right now myself."

"Little is right," Magruder said. "Hell, you couldn't make a mouse groan."

"Hey, fuck you."

"Like I said, with what? Way I hear it, you have to rent a microscope to find it when you want to piss."

Peterson laughed, and Magruder chuckled at his own joke. They were feeling better, to judge from the banter. They'd made it to safety, the general hadn't stomped them flat on the way. If the civilians didn't cooperate, fuck 'em. They could steal their transport and full-wing it to worlds elsewhere.

"What's that on the wall?" Peterson said.

"What? Where?"

Renus tapped Magruder on the shoulder with his carbine. "Over there, to the left."

The three men moved.

"Why the hell don't they have any lights in here? Christo, it's like a tomb."

Magruder pulled his flashlight and pointed it at the wall.

The circle of light thrown by the bright halogen

lamp showed a convoluted and ridged overlay on the wall, grayish, like flattened loops of intestine.

"Some kind of sculpture?" Renus said.

"Oh, fuck. Oh, fuck. Oh, fuck!"

Renus and Magruder turned to look at Peterson. "What?" Magruder demanded.

"I—it's—I've seen this shit before!"

"So?"

"When—when I was on guard duty at the queen's chamber."

"What the hell are you talking about?" Renus wanted to know.

"The fucking alien queen's chamber! This shit is all over the wall in her chamber!"

Magruder shone his light farther along the corridor's wall. The stuff continued, spread so it covered the entire wall from the floor to as far up as the light would shine, all the way to the ceiling.

"Ahh!"

Both Renus and Magruder spun, their carbines pointed at the third man.

"What?!"

Peterson wiped something from his face, a clear, slimy goo.

"What the hell is that?" Renus asked.

Peterson looked up at the ceiling.

Renus and Magruder looked up, too.

# 11

The miracle of modern chemistry failed to put Billie to sleep. She added to the medicine the relaxation drill she'd learned in the hospital but after three rounds of pleading for her muscles to relax she was still awake. Mitch had gone, where she didn't know. And she didn't care.

*Right.*

Fuck this.

Billie stood, exhausted but past the point where she could drop off. Washed her face and looked at herself in the small mirror over the basin. Her image stared back, hollow-eyed, her muscles taut with strain. When Wilks had broken her out of the hospital—so long ago it now seemed—her almost-ash hair had been shoulder length. The hair was still a pale-brown but she'd chopped it off short somewhere along the way. She couldn't even remember when she'd done that. During one of the post-sleep lethargies. If there were an omnipotent god out there somewhere who paid attention to what people did, he must have one hell of a warped sense of humor.

She dried her face under the blower, took a few deep breaths, and left the little room.

Billie walked as though she were a passenger on her own shoulders, along for the ride but not in control. She observed almost distantly her feet taking her back to the communications room. Maybe seeing how other people dealt with monsters might help somehow. And she found herself worried about the little girl she'd seen, a child billions of kilometers and years away. What was her name? Amy?

There must have been a shift change, a different tech was on the board when Billie arrived, a man this time. But he must have had his orders, too.

"Annie said you were here earlier," he said. "C'mon in."

Billie nodded at the man and sat next to him.

The images shifted on the various screens, sometimes people, sometimes test patterns, sometimes information blurring past so fast she couldn't begin to read it. A montage of humanity calling out to itself electronically, sending its voices and pictures out on invisible waves into the galaxy. Is anybody listening? Is anybody there?

A woman appeared on the screen to Billie's left. She was attractive, dark hair chopped short in a spacer's cut, chiseled and even features, thin lips, good cheekbones. She spoke rapidly, her image

without sound. Sweat beaded on her forehead, ran
down her face.

"Who's that?"

The tech glanced over at the picture. He smiled.
"That's Ripley."

"Ripley?"

He looked at her as if she were a not particularly
bright child. "Ellen Ripley. *The* Ripley. She was on
the *Nostromo* and the *Sulaco*. She was there at the
beginning, on LV-426, first contact with the aliens.
Holds the record for long sleep, as far as we can
tell. You been living in a cave the last few years?"

"Yeah, you might say that. What happened to
her?"

The tech fiddled with the control. "Can't get the
sound, sorry. This is a real old 'cast. We catch a few
of them now and then, light-speed being as slow as
it is. Never know what you're gonna pick up. I can
plug it into the computer lip-reader, you want."

"What happened to Ripley?"

The tech shrugged. "Dunno. She was the only
survivor of the *Nostromo*. Basically a buncha truck
drivers who sat down in the wrong place at the
wrong time, got infected. She later went back out
to the colony as an adviser with a crew of Colonial
Marines. The colony was destroyed in a nuclear explosion. Probably they all died. There were some
rumors . . ."

Billie, exhausted, stared at the tech. Waited.

"I had a buddy, used to work for a civilian
biotech division of a major Terran company. He
said Ripley managed to get offworld before the
place blew. Wound up on an old prison world
somewhere. They sent somebody out after her, but

that's where the story ends. A lot of shit got lost after the invasion. Who can say?"

"You seem to know a lot about it."

"Not really. Spears—ah—*General* Spears studies everything available on the aliens. Bunch of it gets routed through here. You pick up stuff."

Billie stared at the woman on the screen. She felt a kind of kinship with her. How had she behaved when she faced the things? Was she alive somewhere? Or blown to atomic dust, the same way Wilks had blasted the aliens' homeworld with nuclear flames? Or worse, webbed to a wall and used as a human incubator for a baby monster?

The image faded. Billie leaned back in the chair and allowed the other vidpixs to wash over her. They were hypnotic, light strobing, low sounds droning her into a kind of somnolence . . .

Without realizing it, Billie dropped into a troubled sleep.

The glob of slime apparently marked Peterson somehow as the first target. He raised his carbine and started blasting, waving it back and forth, spraying a 10mm fan of steel-sheathed lead. The armor-piercing bullets sang as they struck the ceiling, the roar of the exploding propellent smashed against the ears of the three marines, deafening them.

Renus and Magruder brought their weapons up but not in time. The things dropped from the ceiling, peeled away from the convoluted resinous bas-relief sculpture, invisible until they moved.

The first alien fell on Peterson, slammed him to the floor, knocked his weapon away.

Peterson screamed, a wordless bleat, full of terror.

The thing bounded up like a giant grasshopper, Peterson held in its claws like a doll.

"Fuck! Shoot it!" Magruder yelled.

"I can't, Peterson's in the way—!"

"Out, out, get out, move—!"

"Help!" Peterson finally found a word to put into the scream.

The alien holding the man leapt toward the wall, reached it. Another alien—two, three of them— unfolded from the wall right in front of the marines and reached out to grab Peterson. They passed him from claw to claw upward.

"Oh, man!" Renus fired, and the closet alien shattered under the hail of hard metal, spraying yellowish fluid in all directions like a popped water balloon.

"Yaah!" Magruder yelled as some of the acid splashed on his suit, ate small holes in it. He turned, ran.

Renus didn't see Magruder go; he was busy waving his carbine back and forth, filling the corridor with noise and death. Another alien fell, cut in half at the hips. But Peterson was gone, moved up the wall out of sight.

More of the things dropped from the ceiling, sprang from the walls, charged Renus.

"Die, motherfuckers!"

The cyclic rate on the M-41E carbine was, in theory, nearly seven hundred rounds per minute. Slightly more than eleven rounds a second. With the weapon held continuously on full auto, therefore, a hundred-round magazine would be exhausted in a little over nine seconds.

It was the longest nine seconds of Renus's life.

Three heartbeats after the magazine ran dry, one of the things sprang at him, shot that efficient toothed rod from its mouth right down Renus's screaming throat. The scream turned into a choked-off liquid gurgle. The aliens had saved Peterson for implantation but Renus was nothing more than fresh meat. The last thing he did before he died was to trigger the grenade launcher on his carbine. The 30mm explosive shell hit the wall at an angle, bounced upward, and went off somewhere near the ceiling. The explosion washed the corridor with clean fire and deadly shrapnel.

Magruder ran, driven by fear and adrenaline, the acid burns on his suit trailing acrid smoke. The blast wave hit him, he staggered, nearly stumbled, but kept on his feet.

Ahead was a doorway marked Interior Life Support. Magruder reached the door, slapped frantically at the admit panel. The door slid open. He jumped into the room, pressed the closure control, held it until the door slid shut.

"Jesus, Jesus, fuck!" Safe, he was safe, for now. He had to find a way out of here, fast! He looked around frantically.

Something clattered, a rattle of claws on a metal grate.

Magruder looked up. Saw one of the aliens overhead on an expanded aluminum mesh ceiling plate. "Fuck!" He snapped the carbine up and fired. Half a dozen rounds hit the grate, some of them got through to the creature. It fell, a puppet with its strings cut, collapsed on the grating. Acid dripped, burned the grate, the floor beneath it, raising smoke and a stench.

Magruder backed away from the acid rain, slammed into the wall.

Something banged on the door. The thin metal dented inward as if it were no thicker than foil.

"Oh, man!"

A claw came through the wall and stabbed Magruder just above his left kidney. He lurched away from the pain, felt a piece of his back jerked out. He screamed wordlessly in pain. The shock hit him as the blood spewed from the hole in his back. He stumbled through the pool of acid eating away at the floor. His boots began to smoke. His feet took fire, blistered, began to char.

He dropped his weapon, pulled at his boots, burned his hands getting them off.

He leaned against another door opposite the one the things tore at.

The door opened behind and he fell backward.

Looming above him, something. An alien! No, it wasn't a thing, it was a man! Thank God!

Then he saw it was Spears.

"The wages of treason are death," Spears said.

He smiled.

Spears had watched it all. The initial desertion. The frantic ride through the canyons. The entry into the air processor plant. This fool thought he could just steal a crawler and escape. Never even looked for the hidden cameras onboard the stolen property, the cameras that sent every moment of the trip back for Spears to enjoy at his leisure. Every word, every fart, every bump on the frantic ride. Just as the surveillance equipment had picked up the attack only moments ago. True, some of the network had been put out of commission by the drones, webbed over or covered by the resin secretions as they built their nest inside the plant, but plenty of photomutable gel eyes had remained. All of it had been recorded, fed to the computers at Third Base, where the tactics would be broken down and studied, used to extend his knowledge of his alien troops.

The three deserters had panicked, lost it, and that disgusted Spears. Real marines would have used controlled bursts, overlapped their fields of fire, and walked through the drones to safety. But humans were weak, filled with fear, and they lost control. Their emotions damned them. Had three aliens been armed as the deserters, the wild strain would not have been able to touch them. That was what a *real* trooper was, one without fear. One without the emotional entanglements that came from being born of woman. In a way, Spears felt a kinship with the aliens. He had come from an egg and sperm, but had been carried to term without the uncertainty of a living mother.

The marine at his feet—Magruder?—stared up at him. "G-g-general! Th-thank God . . ."

"You fucked up, son. Fouled your jets right across the tubes. Because you are weak. But you served your purpose. Every little bit helps. They'll be watching the recording of that chickenshit run you did for a long time. What not to do. A classic example of bad tactics built on an even worse strategy."

He turned. A pair of troopers in full combat gear

stood nearby. They were nervous, fidgety, the stink of fear rising from them. Not much better than this scum lying on the floor, but at least they obeyed orders. It was what he had to work with, for now.

"I'm done with this," Spears said, waving at Magruder. "The drones are hungry. Give them supper."

Magruder screamed. "No! You can't! Please!" He struggled to rise.

One of the guards opened the door. The aliens were about to break through into the next room, the walls shuddered under their blows.

"Please! Pleeaassee!"

The two marines shoved Magruder toward the door. He stuck his arms and legs out, trying to stop himself. Caught the doorjamb with one hand. His fear gave him strength. He stopped.

Spears kicked out with his boot and smashed Magruder's fingers. Magruder screamed as he slid through into the room. The door slid shut with a grating noise.

Spears watched through the plastic viewplate set in the door as the alien drones breached the wall and stormed into the room. Magruder's voice filtered through the closed door. He kicked at the first alien to reach him, but it was a wasted effort.

Spears turned away. "Let's go," he said. "We're done here."

The two guards practically leapt to obey. That brought another smile to Spears's face. A little example did wonders to keep the troops in line. Yes, sir. Indeed it did.

# 12

Powell paced back and forth in the hold of the cargo ship, his movements quick and nervous. "There were one hundred sixty-eight civilian terraformers," he said. "Men, women, children. Spears gave them to the aliens. The air plant is automatic at this stage, you see, so the people were . . . redundant."

Wilks found that he was standing, his fists clenched.

Powell stopped pacing, turned and faced the sergeant.

"You let him do it."

"I'm not a murderer," Powell said. "Not even Spears."

"I saw you reach for that pistol you carry when you got here," Wilks said.

"But I didn't pull it. I would, I suppose, if I truly thought my own life was in jeopardy."

"And you don't think it is? What the hell do you need, a formal declaration of war?"

Powell chewed on that for a second. "Listen," he said, "I joined the service to do my duty for my planet. I was studying for the priesthood at the time. I planned to finish my training and become a chaplain. It didn't work out. I got sidetracked. So I wound up here. What Spears has done sickens me, but the path to the Light is not by creating more darkness."

Wilks stared at the man. He'd run into guys like Powell before. The military had to have a certain number of medics and religious types. Their bent, because of what they did or who they were before they ever joined up, was usually pacifistic. If you were wounded in battle, you needed somebody to staple you back together, so a surgeon; if you were emotionally burned out, some kind of counselor, though Wilks himself hadn't ever had much use for those, psychologists or faithers. They were necessary, but you didn't want one next to you when the grill flamed on and the other side started shooting. And you didn't want one in charge when your ass was on the line. It wasn't that way with all of them—Wilks had seen medics who would just as soon carve your heart out as smile at you and men of various gods who would cheerfully burn a stadium full of small children if they thought that's what their deity wanted. But Powell wasn't one of those.

And, given the situation, that was bad news.

So what did the man want? Why was he telling Wilks all this?

Abruptly it dawned on Wilks exactly why. Powell was one of those who bought his meat flash-wrapped at the market, or pretended it was soypro—but still ate it. He wasn't a hunter himself but he wasn't above enjoying the taste of the game—once it had been sanitized and neatly packaged. Once the thing had been gutted and the blood drained. He would eat it, but he wouldn't hunt and kill it.

And he at least knew a hunter when he saw one.

Wilks nodded to himself. Fine. He could live with that. He was used to doing the dirty work himself.

The queen was a giant, bigger than other queens. A force of nature, unstoppable, irresistible, like something from an ancient mythos. She was the Destroyer of Worlds, she was the eater of souls, it was foolish to even think of resisting her.

The queen loomed large, four sets of inner jaws opening and extruding like a Chinese puzzle box, able to spear and eat anything from mice to elephants. But she wasn't interested in mice or elephants, she wanted other prey. She wanted—

Billie turned to run, but her feet were mired in the floor, she struggled and could only manage a glacial slow motion, as if she were shod in lead boots, as if she were on the bottom of a deep pool full of thick syrup.

She cried out, kept trying to run, but it was hopeless. She could smell the queen as she drew closer, the sharp, bitter, burned-plastic odor of her

flowed out in waves to envelop Billie. The stench of
bodies a-rot for years in some dead and fishless
sea curled over Billie, a pustulent and blackened
breaker with bloody red foam about to crash
down . . .

*Do not be afraid,* the queen said. Her voice was
soothing, a melody from childhood, the tones of a
mother comforting a frightened baby. *I love you. I
want you. I need you.*

"No!" Billie screamed. She'd heard it before. She
knew it was a lie. She struggled to move in her personal amber, a prehistoric fly waiting for the hand
of Death, a doomed insect waiting for Eternity to
smother her.

*I love you. Come. Let me touch you . . .*
A cold claw gripped Billie's shoulder.


"No!"

"Take it easy!" the tech said. He stood next to
her, his hand on her shoulder. "It's okay. You're just
dreaming."

Billie blinked, trying to make the transition from
*there* to here.

"I know how it is," the tech said. "I dream about
her, too."

Billie stared, unable to bring up words.

"Tell the medics. They've got some stuff that
helps."

"Nothing helps," Billie said. "I've been dealing
with this since I was ten. It's only a matter of time
until the dreams finally come true."

Outside the com room there came a sound as if
someone were thumping down the hallway on

metal boots. Billie was sure she knew exactly who it was.

Ah, shit. What was she going to do about Mitch? Even as pissed as she'd been when they fought, she still felt that pull, that energy. Fuck, call it what it was. That *love*.

Damn.

As they were leaving the complex, Spears took a short detour through one of the newer egg chambers. A mere dozen eggs rested here on the alien-constructed floor, all fairly fresh, only a couple of days old. He had surveillance gear everywhere; he knew there was no danger of these units hatching anytime soon. Plus, the doors, left open deliberately so the drones could move the eggs unimpeded, still worked. He had a trooper crank the doors shut, so he could be in the room for a few moments without interruption from nervous drone egg-tenders.

He liked to do this, visit the eggs. The rubbery, fleshy shells with the flower-petal lips still clenched tightly together, protecting their precious cargo, they touched something in Spears. He was not a man given to deep introspection, no navel picker to worry over the unchangeable past or unborn future, he was a doer, not a ponderer; still, there was a cold and merciless beauty to be found here. These were unborn warriors out of the greatest warriors man had ever met. And Spears was a man of war.

With two guards standing nervously alert, Spears walked to the nearest egg, squatted, put one hand out to feel the roughness of the living container.

You could drop this little closed barrel off a tall building in standard gee and it would bounce like a plastic ball without damaging the tiny occupant. Spears knew, because he'd had it done. In the variable gravity room the scientists had built, they'd done more than a few such experiments. The eggs were tough. Even under three gees they still maintained their integrity. They could be cut, were the knife sharp enough, but the wielder had best be very quick—piercing the outer wall of an egg would get the cutter a face full of acid spray even more potent than that in the grown creatures' blood. Nature had been lavish in her protection of the aliens' birth packaging. And the first-stage babies were hardy little devils, too.

Spears grinned, stroked the egg as if it were the head of a faithful dog. The alien queens could reproduce in a kind of modified parthenogenesis, and the drones were mostly neuters. There were some males—the labbos had found a few—and indications were that there could be a battlelike sexual intercourse between the two sexes. The available males, when they reached some critical number, fought each other to the death, leaving only a single survivor, who then lay claim to the queen. She made him work for it, slammed him all over the place, and if he survived this battering, worse than the fights with the other males, the queen would submit to his advances.

The male's triumph would be short-lived. Within seconds after this hard-contested mating was consummated, the queen would kill the hapless male. The scientists babbled on about genetic diversity and such, but it didn't matter. If there weren't any males around, the queen could do it herself. And if there weren't any queens around, one of the drones would undergo what the scientists called a hormone storm; when it was done, the drone would be a queen.

Spears shook his head. Goddamned efficient bastards. Just what a commander in the field needed. You could hatch your own army in a few months and as long as one of 'em stayed alive, you could start over again when those got killed.

The troopers moved around, Spears could feel their fear. He grinned again, partly because he knew they were scared and he wasn't, partly because growing down his uniform pants leg was a fairly solid erection. As long as he squatted here, stroking the egg, it didn't show. He chuckled at his own hormone storm. That didn't happen much anymore, he'd managed to sublimate his sexual drives into more important things, but the little head did rear now and again. Not that he found sex unpleasant, no, that wasn't the problem, just that it took too much time and energy to indulge in it these days. Course, when he'd been younger, he thought he would live forever and he would fuck anything with a hole and a pulse and even the latter wasn't strictly necessary. And he'd learned something from the very first time he'd ever done it, something very important.

He laughed at the memory. Ah, Gunnery Sergeant Brandywine. Whatever happened to her?

Colonial Marine Cadet Spears at fifteen was still two years away from his first hitch, though he'd already gotten three Corps tattoos. Gunny Brandywine was his small-arms instructor, she was probably twice his age, tough as a boot sole, and could drill the eye out of a ship rat at twenty paces with a carbine or a handgun, you pick which eye. She wore her black hair chopped short in a spacer's buzz, had a rangy, tight frame, flat pectoral muscles and no breasts to speak of, and abs Spears would die to have himself. A lean, mean fighting machine, Gunny was, a strong and deadly female. He'd watched her in the showers a couple of times, carefully keeping his back turned so she wouldn't see the short-arm salute she was causing. Christ, he was so hard sometimes it stood nearly straight up.

He didn't think she'd noticed, but one afternoon after a session in the gym with the autoboxer, he'd found himself alone in the shower with her. As usual, his dick was trying to go ballistic, and he kept fiddling with the water's temp control, as if it were malfunctioning, so he could keep his erection out of her sight.

She shut her shower off and started to leave. Good.

But her footsteps on the wet plastic tiles went the wrong way. He could see her peripherally when she reached out and slapped him on the shoulder. "Come on, cadet. You might as well learn how to use that."

Spears thought of himself as a marine already, tough, unflappable, cool under stress, but he felt himself go red. "Excuse me?"

"You've been wanting to stick that in me for weeks, kid. In my quarters, five minutes, you can give it a shot." She turned and padded away. He watched the muscular roll of her buttocks, unable to breathe he was so scared.

But it had been fine. Gunny was practiced, she had obviously broken in more than a few first-timers, and she was patient.

The first round took maybe three seconds until he discharged his weapon. Five strokes, no more. It was great, but he knew enough to realize it hadn't done anything for her. He started to apologize. "Oh, man, I'm sorry, I—!"

"Forget it, cadet. I know how you young guys are. Besides, that didn't even take the edge off you. Here. Give me that."

The next three hours were a wonder to Cadet Spears. Sure, he had beat-off plenty, but it didn't feel anywhere close to as good as what Gunny Brandywine taught him that afternoon. Amazing things.

In the end, the most useful thing of all was patience. He was a hot-shot cadet, always rushing, always in a hurry, like life was a race he had to finish first. He couldn't wait to be on active duty. Gunny taught him how to wait.

They were on her bed, reconnected for the fifth time, she on her back, one leg drawn up, foot hooked over his ass, he on his side, pumping fast.

"Slow down, mister."

"Huh?"

She reached out, caught his hip with one hand, slowed his movement.

"When you're on the handgun range and you get an in-your-face pop-up target, what do you do?"

"Pointshoot, triple tap, two in the heart, one in the head," Spears said, as if he were in class. Which, he realized much later, he was.

"Right. Slow will get you killed in that combatsit. But if you get a pop-up at fifty meters, do you react the same way?"

He continued his motion at the speed she had set.

"No, ma'am," he said. "You take deliberate aim using your sights and squeeze off two to the torso."

"Ah, that feels good." She grinned, looked at him. Raised her leg so her toes pointed at the ceiling. "Now, back in the combat scenario, explain your actions."

"Pointshooting is inaccurate at long range. Accuracy is more important than speed in that situation. Shoot too fast and miss, the enemy might not. Better to be slow and certain."

"Push a little harder now, and a little faster." She bent her knee, brought it down close to her face. "Good. Put your finger here. Rub this way. Mmm."

He was getting close again. But he forced himself to hold his pacing where she wanted it.

"Life is like the range, cadet. There's a time to hurry and a time to go slow. Learning when to do the right thing at the right time is as important as anything you'll ever learn, you got that?"

He nodded. Drawing close to his release yet again, he would have agreed with anything she said, but on some level, he did understand the lesson. It was a unique teaching method.

"*Now* you go fast. Move, cadet. Move!"

He obeyed. It was one hell of a teaching method.

· · ·

Spears came back to himself. Patted the egg and stood, his sexual excitement cooled. A less patient man than himself might have missed this whole opportunity to develop an invincible army. If Gunny Brandywine were still alive, she'd be a crone, pushing eighty, easy, but it would be interesting to see her. To show her how well her lesson had taken. And what the hell, maybe to fuck her once for old times' sake.

"Let's move out, marines."

He wouldn't have to tell these men that twice.

# 13

"The queen has learned to obey the general," Powell said. He leaned against a bulkhead, staring at the floor.

"Obey him?" Wilks said.

They'd been in the little ship a long time, Wilks was beginning to feel stiff and cramped, but he wanted to hear as much of it as Powell could get out before they had to break this off.

"Oh, yes. Spears started training her like a dog. Used his cigar lighter. He'd have a trooper with a flamethrower roast an egg while the queen watched. After she calmed down, he'd put a human into the testing cage with her. When she went for the bait, he'd pop the cigar lighter on and hold it next to another egg. The queen picked it up fast. You could leave a man in with her and a dozen drones for hours and none of them would touch him. She's not stupid, the queen.

"It seems odd, though," Powell continued, "that the queen will sacrifice the drones without a second thought but that she'll obey Spears to protect the eggs."

Wilks shrugged. "She's an alien. What drives her doesn't drive us. Maybe her responsibility ends when the damned things hatch."

"That's what Spears thinks. But she controls the drones. Telepathically, empathically, we don't have the sophisticated gear here to be sure exactly how, but it isn't with sound or odors or any visual signals we can detect. We've run tests where the drone was a klick away in an airtight chamber, no possible way it could see or hear the queen, and Spears made it do what he wanted."

"You have more than one queen," Wilks said.

Powell blinked. "How do you know that?"

"Somebody is laying the eggs in the air processor. Unless you're ferrying the queen from here back and forth."

"No, you're right. We put one egg from this nest over there. Spears did it himself. There are a score of drones there now tending the young queen."

Wilks shook his head in disgust. "Spears doesn't know what the hell he is messing with here."

"He thinks he does. And he's done more with them than anybody else, Wilks. Last month he took a dozen of the things out and had them marching in close order drill. He's taught several of them how to hold a modified M-69 machine gun and had them shooting the weapon."

"Jesus."

"Yes. It's Maggie's Drawers for accuracy, they can't hit anything smaller than a wall even at close range, but still."

Wilks nodded. A monster with a machine gun. The only advantage men had in battle with these things was their weaponry. If they were armed as well as human troops, they'd be unstoppable.

"The drones are stupid," Powell said. "But even a chimp can be trained to shoot fairly straight. And we think the queen's connection with the drones gives her the ability to see what she sees. And the queen is probably as smart as we are, according to the psychologists."

"Buddha fucking Christ."

"Crude, but apt."

Wilks stood, paced across the room. "But— what's the point? Earth is history. When we left there, it was already nearly overrun. A few more years and everybody there will be dead. A few clean neutron bombs after that would sterilize the place. All this cowboy shit is stupid."

"This isn't about saving the Earth or anybody on it," the major said. "It's about Spears and his ideas of personal glory. Or something. I don't know what, for sure."

Wilks nodded. "All right. Let's get to the bottom line here, Major."

Powell sighed. "Enough people have died, Sergeant. This has to end. Spears is at the air processor plant. There's a magnetic storm heading this way, sunspot activity on the primary is up. Spears will be delayed some hours, maybe even a day or two before he can lift and return to base. We need to begin our preparations now."

Wilks nodded. "All right."

"Mitch?"

The door to his room was open. He was half machine now, but the android part of him was programmed for sleep, to enhance his human characteristics. He lay on a pallet on his back, a sheet covering him to the chest.

"Come in, Billie."

The room's lighting was dim, and he was barely visible as she approached the pallet. She stopped two meters away. "I'm sorry," she said. "I shouldn't have said what I said."

He remained lying down, his hands under his head. He stared straight up at the ceiling. "I can understand that you were upset."

"It didn't give me the right to behave that way. It's just that—" she stopped.

"Just that what?"

She turned slightly, so she was looking at the back wall and not directly at him. "It's all so confusing," she said. "I thought I had gotten past it, about your being an artificial person. That it didn't matter."

"But it does matter, doesn't it?"

Her sigh was almost a sob. "When we came out of the sleep chambers on the way here, you seemed so cold. So distant. I didn't understand it. I still don't understand it. What happened, Mitch? Did you change? Or was it me?"

Now he sat up, the sheet draping down around his waist, covering the metal skeleton and revealing his bare upper body. He looked human to her in this light. Was human, she reminded herself, but not quite the same as she was.

"They made us to be as much like humans as possible. We're as far away from first-generation synthetics as they were from robots. Almost human.

"Funny, there were rumors we heard when we were still damp from the vats—the next generation of synthetics could not only pass for human among wombfolk, they would be born thinking they *were* human. Memory tapes of childhood, family, full implant blocks of internal workings, anatomically perfect right down to a dye in the circulation fluid so it would look like human blood to a naked eye.

"They would not only look like naturals, they would believe they were naturals. There would be inbuilt Laws of Function, of course, but the new APs would simply think they were personal ethics. They'd have the same energy requirements, ability to process food, oxygen, normal elimination, same natural cycles. For all practical purposes, they would be people, save that they couldn't reproduce, and they would be stronger, faster, and more durable."

"Mitch—"

"Of course," he went on, ignoring her interruption, "the question that immediately arose was: What's the point? If you want real people, why not make them the old-fashioned way, parent or artificial wombs? And the answer was that they would be expendable. Able to do the dirty and dangerous work that real men didn't want to do. Radiation disposal, exploration on hostile worlds, pressure rescue, suicide missions for whatever reasons.

"The new androids would be perfect. Acceptable in polite society, able to move without upsetting the most delicate sensibilities, but throwaways. Instant third-class citizens—no, not even citizens, but property, slaves, loyal as dogs, ready to leap at the proper command."

"Jesus, Mitch—"

"I'm not finished yet. But to get to those happy models, they had to experiment. Stir in the proper emotions so the passers-for-human would laugh at the right spots, cry when appropriate, even fall in love when necessary. So, here we are, you and I. It worked. My fake hormones did what they were supposed to do and I fell for you. Only thing is, there's enough of me outside the emotional part that I can understand it apart from the feelings."

Billie turned and looked at him. "And you resent me for it," she said finally.

"No. Not you. See, I do love you. But I resent them for making me this way. They didn't give me any experience, any guidance, any way of dealing with this whole thing rationally."

Billie smiled, small, sad, but a smile nonetheless.

His eyes were better than hers. He saw the expression. "Something funny about this?"

She heard the anger in him. "In a way. Nobody ever gave me any guidance or way of dealing with this 'whole thing' either, Mitch. Love and logic don't go together. You're looking for a nice clean path to walk. It doesn't happen that way very often among us 'naturals,' either. Love is usually messy, cluttered, sometimes painful and just plain awful."

"At least you had a choice," he said.

"What makes you think so? We don't get to choose any more than you do in some things."

"You could have walked away. You didn't have to love me."

"I could have walked away from you but I couldn't walk away from my *feelings*. That's why I can't just bail out now. I could leave but what I feel for you would stay with me."

"This is beyond my capabilities to understand," he said.

"Welcome to the club."

The silence stretched long between them. If only he had told her before they'd begun. If only she had known. She wasn't a bigot, she could have gotten past it, could have accepted him.

*Really? Are you sure about that, Billie? Are you?*

There was the damning part of it. She wasn't sure.

Not at all.

Spears sat in the ship, waiting for the goddamned storm to pass. Stupid, he'd known the solar magnetic activity was up, there had been swirls forecast, he should have destroyed the traitors and hustled his ass back to base. They could have beaten it, if they had hurried.

Well. Done was done, no point in crying over a broken plan. Best he make use of the time. There were some combat scenarios he wanted to run; the compsim unit had the latest learned-commands the alien troops had assimilated logged into it. They weren't a crack fighting unit yet, not by any means, but they were getting there. It was just a matter of time. And when they were ready, nothing in the universe could stand against them. Spears's word would carry more weight than God's when he had these troops whipped into shape. Yes, indeed.

Just a matter of time.

# 14

A man carrying a durasteel fire ax hurried across the open space, moving crouched. "Over here," he called out.

After a moment a second man came into view, this one carrying a small shovel with a green plastic handle. Both of them were dirty, their clothes torn and worn. The first man had on a leather jacket that had probably once been black but was now a sun-bleached pale gray. The second man wore a dark blue nylon or synlon windbreaker with a hood.

"You sure about this?" Nylon asked.

"No, I ain't sure," Leather replied. "But if it's true, we're in fat town for sure. C'mon, dig."

The men were next to a collapsed building. The arched doorway immediately behind them stood upright in the rubble and looked to be made of steel—there were patches of orange-brown rust on the metal and a few twisted rods extending from it.

"Man, it'll take hours to get down far enough," Nylon said.

"Yeah, but if there *is* a military food cache there, we're talking about maybe a ton of canned food and *barrels* of clean water. We can retire to the Hidden Underground and never have to worry about bugs again."

Nylon lifted a shovelful of debris and tossed it to one side. "Hidden Underground. You believe that shit?"

"I believe I can buy the prettiest woman in the burg with five cans of unspoiled edibles and ten armed guards with a hundred. With a truck full of military-issue protein, I can damn sure find out if there's an HU. Shut up and fucking dig." Leather used the ax as if it were a rake, moving shards of brick and stone aside.

"Okay, okay. Where's Petey?"

"Standing watch, moron. Up on the tower."

Nylon glanced up at a pockmarked building across the street. A segment of the structure extended up three or four stories, carved like some ancient rock formation, only not by wind and rain but by bombs and fire.

"I don't see 'im."

"You're not supposed to see him, he's supposed to see you, and anybody else who might come strolling along. You didn't think I was gonna be rooting around out here in the open without covering my ass, did you?"

Nylon shrugged, said nothing, went back to digging. With the two of them scraping at the rubble, anything they said was covered by the sounds of their work.

"Amy, what are you doing?" The speaker was unseen, his voice almost a whisper.

"Videoing, Uncle Burt. You can hear everything they say and they look real close in the camera, see?"

"You shouldn't be out here, Amy, you know that. Your mother would—uh-oh. Here give me the cam."

The viewpoint shifted, there was a quick disorienting flash of the ground and a small girl's leg, then the picture steadied on the two diggers again, the angle slightly higher.

"Nobody moves," came a deep and unseen voice. A second later, a tall man in GF camo gear stepped into sight, a softslug shotgun held at his hip. The soldier pointed his weapon at the two diggers.

"Oh, fuck," Nylon said. "Where the hell is Petey?"

"Look," Leather said, "there's plenty to go around. We ain't greedy, we'll split it with you."

The soldier laughed. Waved the shotgun. "There's nothing down there, scatcats. We put out that rumor to catch guys like you."

"Motherfucker," Leather said.

"Oh, man, oh, man!" Nylon said. "You're bug feeders! Fucking bug feeders!"

The soldier took a step and slapped Nylon across the temple with the barrel of the shotgun, hard enough to knock him to his knees but not so hard as to put him out. "Don't call us that, scum. Never say that. We serve the queens. It is an honor. An honor, you hear? But you wouldn't understand that. You aren't among the Chosen." The soldier glanced to his left. "Simmons, King, front and center."

Two more soldiers, also armed with shotguns, came into view. Walking ahead of them, a third man, his hands cuff-taped behind him.

"Oh, man, Petey," Nylon said.

"You're not feeding me to the goddamn bugs!" Leather said. He threw the ax at the first soldier, turned and ran.

Simmons and King snapped their weapons up. "I got him!" one of them yelled. "Cover the others!"

The speaker fired his weapon. The charge caught the running man's left ankle. He managed one more step and then collapsed when his weight came down on the shattered joint. He screamed.

The ax didn't do any apparent damage to the first soldier, who said, "Go get him. I've got these two."

The two soldiers moved to grab Leather.

"The queen will be pleased with these three," the first soldier said. "She will smile upon us." He looked around the clearing, what had once been a busy street in a major city.

The viewpoint shifted. "Go, Amy," the unseen Uncle Burt said, his voice urgent. "Go, go!"

The image vanished. The scanners cycled, looking for another broadcast.

Seated before the now-blank screen, Billie was drenched in sweat, her heart pounding.

"Lot of them went over like that," the female tech said. Annie, Billie remembered. "Not enough they have drones out hunting people. Now they got traitors doing their work for them, too. Hard to imagine why somebody would do that."

Billie sighed, and it was almost a sob. Yeah. It was hard to imagine, but there it was. Jesus. How could anybody sink that low? Jesus.

The familiar weight of the 10mm carbine in his hands felt good. He wasn't in field armor, but Wilks also had four spare magazines strapped around his waist. Five hundred rounds ought to be plenty.

Powell had gone off to the computer center to do the kind of thing he could do, fiddle with controls. Didn't matter, Wilks would manage the hot work, it was the one thing the marines had taught him well.

Ahead, the doorway to the communications shack loomed. Wasn't even closed. Of course, they didn't have any reason to worry about security. Or at least, they hadn't until now.

When Wilks stepped into the small room, he saw Billie sitting in one of the chairs, staring at a blank screen. Next to her was a female tech.

"Back away from the console," Wilks said.

Billie looked at him. "Wilks. What—?"

The tech started to touch a control.

"Unh-uh, lady, you don't want to do that." He waved the carbine at her. "Roll the chair back and stand up slowly."

The tech, unarmed, did as she was told.

"Wilks!"

"Come stand over here, Billie."

She shook her head in puzzlement, but complied.

He opened up on the console first, then shifted his hip point up and raked the screens. He was wearing canal suppressor buttons so the sound was muted for him, but the two women covered their ears with their hands. The tech screamed. Thirty rounds were plenty. The hard plastic chipped and shattered, delicate biocircuits shorted out, and the flat screens starred and ran out of image, turning a dark gray.

Long-range communications at Third Base were history, at least for a while. There would be radio and Doppler on the crawlers and ships, of course, some of it capable of reaching over the near horizon to Spears, but if he hurried, nobody would get to those. Or if they did, it wouldn't matter.

"Wilks, what the *fuck* are you doing?"

"Staging a coup. Or a mutiny. When Spears comes back, he is going to be relieved of command. Powell is taking over."

"Shit, that pussy?" the tech said. "Spears will chew him to pieces."

"If it was just him, yeah, probably. But there's a few troopers who don't want to become monster food, they're on Powell's side. And then there's me. Which team you want to be on, sister?"

The tech licked her lips. Sighed. "I'm with you. Sooner or later everybody fucks up. That happens, you go into the hive. I'd rather swallow a bullet than an egg."

Wilks nodded. "Come on, then. Tell me about communications elsewhere on the station."

"What is the situation on the storm, trooper?"

The man shook his head, obviously nervous. "Still swirling, sir. We can't hope to lift for at least another three hours." The trooper swallowed. "Sir."

Spears nodded. Not much he could do about the

weather here. On some planets, decent-sized
worlds, there were measures that could be taken
with surface meteorology. A climate-controlled
world wouldn't have your troops bogged down in
mud or freezing in snow at the wrong time. A good
commander had to think of such things. Many a
battle had been lost not to the enemy but to a freak
rain or heat low. A kamikaze—a Divine Wind—had
once saved the old Terran empire of the Nihonese
from an invasion by sea; better weather at the start
would have tilted major engagements of the Civil
War toward the South; the Australian Wars, the
Acturian Police Action, the Berringetti Conflict, the
outcomes had been affected in all these by a capri-
cious natural ecology. How galling it must be to
know you were superior in strength and numbers,
had tactical advantages in terrain and matériel,
and were a better strategist, only to be defeated by
a monsoon. Could make an atheist believe in gods,
that kind of shit.

Spears nodded to himself. "What about communications with the base?"

"Negative, sir. Even the LOS transmitters can't
punch through the swirls. Sorry."

"Not your fault, marine. Carry on."

Spears turned away from the communications
man. They were in the plant's south dock, a forti-
fied and secured area the alien drones were unlikely to be able to penetrate, even if their queen
would allow them to try. The place rang hollow
under Spears's gravity-augmented boot heels as he
walked to the intercom sensor and waved it on. His
men were clustered around their craft, talking in
low tones. Scared shitless of the aliens. As well

they should be. "Computer, put visual of the queen on-air."

The holoproj flowered in front of the general. Four cameras, four different views of the young queen, busy pumping out fresh eggs four levels below where Spears now stood. "Good girl," he said, smiling. "Just keep those troopers coming. Computer, ignite the floor burner in the chamber."

"Burner tube is blocked," the computer said.

Spears allowed his smile a bit more wattage. Had to give it to the queen, she never stopped trying. Her drones had paved over the burner, probably four feet of the rock spittle covered the training device. "Clear the burner tube."

After a moment, a faint orange glow began in one corner of the chamber, quickly climbing through the spectrum from dull to bright. A thin blue line flashed, speared through the overlay with the sharpness of a laser beam, hard-edged in the dim room.

"Tube cleared," the computer said.

The queen had noticed and Spears would bet megacredits to mouse turds she knew what was coming. "Light the burner. Half-second burst only."

A blast of flammable gas roared up to splash against the ceiling, a single hot ejaculation that cut off while the circle of fire still painted a yellow-orange circle on the ridged overlay.

The queen looked at the vanishing fire, then swiveled her great emplated head to look directly at one of the cameras focused on her.

Spears chuckled. She knew it was there, knew he was watching her. "Computer, give the queen an image of the pulse-paint room. And put me onscreen so she can see me, too."

The projection swirled into life in the chamber, the details hard to make out from where Spears watched his own holoproj. But he knew the queen could see it well enough. The queen looked at the image, then back at the camera. Opened her mouth, hissed an acknowledgment at the tiny version of the general floating in the air before her.

Spears nodded. "Very wise, little mother." He turned away from the screen, looked at his human troops. "Gizhamme, Ceman, Kohm, front and center. We're going to the ID room."

The three men traded glances, but hurried to obey.

Very good, for troops about to be outmoded. They followed their commander.

Billie followed Wilks down the corridor. "We'll get you a gun, Billie," he said. "Soon as we get control of the situation on this level."

"What exactly are we doing here?" she asked.

"Taking sides," he said. "Powell has given me a list of men and women we can depend on to lean our way. And the transponder coordinates of the troops who are likely to stay loyal to Spears. We're going to round up and detain the general's supporters. Then when he comes home, we won't have so much to worry about. We take him down, flush all this demented shit away, and live happily ever after."

"You've said that before," Billie said.

"I'm still working on it, kid. Give me a little time. Earth wasn't built in a day, you know." He grinned.

Billie returned the smile. She was tired and had a lot on her mind, but she had no trouble buying into this scenario. If they didn't do something about the madman running this base, he would kill them all sooner or later. Win or lose, this had to be better than the alternative.

"Do you know where Mitch is?"

"If he's where he's supposed to be, yeah. He'll be rigging an override in life support's auxiliary control by now."

"Why there?"

"Well, the base is military, so there are modular fail-safes all over for air and gravity and heat and light, but if the mains go down, the emergency doors shut tight. Our side has the new override codes, their side won't. They'll be bottled up unless we let them out."

"Nice trick."

"I thought so. Powell's idea. He's not much of a field soldier, but he's not bad behind a console."

Wilks pulled a small device from the cro-patch on his belt, looked at it. "Ah, here we go. There are five of the bad guys just ahead, in the queen's antechamber. Stay behind me until we get the field of fire on them."

"Copy that."

"Feels good to be moving, doesn't it?"

Billie nodded. "Yeah. I hate to say it, but you're right."

"Hey, that wasn't so hard. You should practice saying it more often, it'll get easier."

"First you have to *be* right once in a while, Wilks."

"I like you, too, kid. Come on."

• • •

Spears held the pulse-paint gun five centimeters away from the drone's skull. It had its mouth closed, but he could smell its carrion breath. It would just as soon kill him as look at him, he knew, but it would not. The queen understood what would happen to her and her precious eggs if any of her drones so much as laid a claw on Spears. It was all about control, about power, and Spears had both. It had taken time and effort to find the aliens' Achilles heel, but once he had found it, he kept his arrow aimed right at it. It was their only weakness, and he knew how to exploit it.

The general waved the paint gun back and forth. The paint was actually microencapsulated grains of tritium in an acidic solution. The gun was programmed and sequenced so it would spray the correct number. The gun hummed as it forced the glowing slurry out under pressure. The material's color was also computer-controlled; this trooper would become a member of the Greens in another two seconds. There were seven corps in his New Colonial Marines, one for each color of the rainbow. As of now, he had less than a score in each of the corps, not much of an army per se, but one had to start somewhere.

The number 19 etched itself into the drone's exoskeleton, deep enough so it wouldn't rub off, not so deep as to cause any damage. In the night, the radioactive tritium would be visible for a long way; in daylight, the number still stood out against the dark gray of the alien's skull. Under an augstrobe, the paint would pulse, like a sighting laser, each number blinking rapidly so a field commander in the air could visually acquire and pinpoint his men from even farther away than usual, if need be.

Spears would put a copy of the skull ID on the back of the head in a moment. For now, he leaned back slightly and observed his work. "Welcome to the Colonial Marines, son."

The drone did not react, but Spears fancied that on some deep if murky level, it understood.

Spears slapped the thing on the skull. It was cold, smooth, slightly clammy to his touch. "Now you stand still, marine, while I get the backside."

Spears was aware of his three human troopers watching him as he moved around the platform.

"Jesus Christ," one of the men whispered. He must have thought Spears couldn't hear him. But the general heard. He made a mental note of it. Disloyalty was everywhere. Even among the so-called best of his human troops.

He put one hand out and touched the alien's skull to steady himself as he brought the paint gun up. Disloyalty wouldn't be a problem with these soldiers. They did what their queen said without question, without hesitation. And Spears controlled the queens.

Glowing green etched itself into the hardness of his new recruit's head. *Semper fidelis,* Spears thought. That was never more true—this marine would always be faithful. It would be the perfect soldier when Spears got finished with it.

Perfect.

# 15

One of Powell's supporters arrived right after Wilks and Billie, also armed with a carbine. Between the two of them, they had no trouble capturing the four men and one woman whose transponders IDed them as Spears loyalists. At least according to Powell. Wilks didn't much like trusting the major, but in this case, the choice was easy enough. At least Powell wasn't homicidal.

"What's the scat, Sarge?" one of the captured troops said.

"Changing of the guard," Wilks answered. "To keep it simple, here's the drill: Spears is out. Powell is in. Any problems with that?"

The five troopers glanced around. And at the weapon Wilks held across his chest in port-arms position.

"You breaking a few regs here, Sarge," one of the women said. "Spears will cut you a new asshole."

"Yeah? How long you figure before you trip over one of those regs and wind up feeding the general's little pets?" Wilks asked her. "You know some of the people webbed in there, don't you?" He waved at the reinforced wall to his left. The queen's chamber was on the other side.

He could see them weighing it. If Spears came back and assumed command, they would be in deep shit if they played along with this. He was not a forgiving man. On the other hand, if Powell was the new honcho in charge, he wouldn't give them to the aliens. A smart marine would sit tight and wait to see which way the current flowed.

Then again, Wilks thought, a smart marine would have figured out that it was only a matter of time before they all went into the chambers as protein supplies for Spears's new and improved troops. Like the three who deserted and ran, only to find themselves out of the intake and into the combustion chamber. And it wasn't as though Colonial Marine line troopers were galaxy-renowned for their high intelligence.

Then *again*, he had the gun. Even a stupid marine usually figured that possibly dying in the future was better than for sure dying right *now*.

"Looks like it's your show, Sarge," one of them said.

"That it is. Let's take a little stroll to assembly, what say?"

The lights blinked out, followed by the sound of pressure doors dropping into place. That would be Bueller. The emergency lighting popped on almost immediately. Half a second, no more. Unfortunately, that half a second was enough time for the largest of the troopers to think he could take advantage of the darkness. He jumped at Wilks.

Wilks's first reaction was to shoot the sucker. He was big, but slow, and he had plenty of time to cap one off into the man. But blowing away marines, however misguided their sense of duty, didn't appeal much to somebody who'd spent most of his life in the corps. He'd done it before, he hadn't liked it.

Wilks sidestepped to his left, swung his foot up in a spring kick, caught the charging man high in the belly. Stole his wind just long enough for the second kick, this one to the man's right leg, next to his knee. The attacker's leg buckled, the ligaments and cartilage torn, and he collapsed onto the deck, cursing.

The Powell-loyal trooper brought his weapon to eye level and prepared to fire on the other captured troops.

"Negative!" Wilks yelled. "Don't shoot! There's no need."

The armed man glanced at Wilks.

"My men are in control of life support," Wilks said, making it up as he went along. "If anything happens to me, you lose heat and air, you're bottled up here without the exit codes. Anybody want to choke to death, taking me out is the way to do it." To prove he wasn't worried, he lowered his own weapon.

The four troopers still standing looked at each other uneasily. It was one thing to catch a round in battle and go fast, another to lie on a floor sucking air that had gone foul with $CO_2$. Not a pleasant way to die.

"Nobody is gonna do nothin', Sarge. You call it."

"That's good. Help bimboboy up and let's move."

The four moved to help the wounded marine.

Well. So far, so good. He hoped it would all go so easy.

Wilks seemed to have things well planned and under control, Billie saw. As they moved through the station, Wilks used a magnetic card and a keypad code to open the pressure doors. Once, there were three men waiting on the other side of a door, but Wilks herded some of the captives through first, their hands raised, to advise the marines of the situation. The threat was simple: Surrender your weapons or freeze in the dark trying to breathe. He must have forgotten that he was going to give Billie a gun, because she hadn't collected one yet. Not that there were many guns around. A couple of carbines, some pistols from various guards. Apparently Spears didn't like his men running around the base armed. Probably a good idea, it would have been too tempting to take a shot at him.

By now they had collected about thirty people, about half of them loyal to Spears, according to Wilks, who seemed to know how to tell the difference with some kind of electronic device he carried. Interesting.

"Where are we going?" Billie asked him.

"Central Assembly," he said. "Gotta sort these guys out as to ours and his. Powell says there are a hundred seventy-five marines, forty-eight scientists and medicos, a couple of androids, and fifteen workbots here. Spears has a short platoon, twenty-five men, with him. We can't have anybody running around loose who might short-circuit things."

"A lot of people to find," she said. "Couple hundred and then some."

"Used to be more. Powell says there were almost five hundred marines assigned to this base. Want to guess where the other half of them went?"

Billie swallowed, her throat suddenly dry.

"Between them and the colonists, Spears has given the aliens more than four hundred people."

"God."

"More like the Devil, I'd say, if I were inclined to believe in such things, kid."

Billie blinked and thought about somebody who would give that many of his fellow humans up to such a horrible death. He had to be crazy.

"Yeah, he's that," Wilks said.

She hadn't realized she'd spoken it aloud.

"But don't worry about it. We're going to shut it down. Powell says the medicos on his side know how to put the corraled aliens down fast; we can shut them off like lights"—he snapped his fingers—"that quick. Soon as we get Spears's loyalists locked up, we turn this place into an alien graveyard. The air processing plant is a little harder, but we can work something out, worst comes to worst, we'll just nuke the whole place."

One of the captured marines overheard this. "You can't do that!" she said. "The air plant is worth billions! And we need the oxy!"

"Sister, this planetoid is a wash. Even if we cook the plant crispy, some of those things might be dug in. They can survive a long time without food, without water, even without air. They could hibernate for *years*, just waiting for some fool to come along and be dinner. The best we can do is kill all those we can spot and then bail out. On sterile ships, too."

"You would let the Earth be overrun by these things and destroy the only means of combating them?"

Wilks looked at the woman as if she had grown fangs. "You buy that shit?" he said. "You think Spears is gonna drop down and clean up the whole fucking planet with a couple of hundred tame monsters?"

"He knows what he's doing," she said.

Wilks just shook his head. "Move, sister. You believe that, you're as crazy as he is."

Spears had learned over the years that circumstances often dictated events in a way that was beyond human control. Since the magnetic storm had caught them, there was no help for it, save to make the best of the enforced grounding. He'd worked computer scenarios, painted new trooper IDs, and now stood in a makeshift shooting range, provided by an unused corridor with a soakplate at the end as a backstop. It wasn't state of the art, no holographic attackers who would crumple and fall realistically when hit by computer-tuned and augmented weaponry; still, it would serve. A trooper stood out of sight through an open doorway ten meters down the corridor from where Spears was. With his pistol holstered, Spears called out, "Throw!" and went for his weapon.

The hidden trooper tossed an industrial-sized food can into the corridor so it entered at eye level and climbed in a lazy arc toward the high ceiling. The can was bright red plastic, as big as a small wastebasket, and it rose slowly in the reduced gravity of the corridor—micromanagement of gee was possible if you had a good programmer working the generators and plenty of time on his hands to route the flux lines.

Spears fired. The caseless round punched into the can as it reached its apex. In the lowered gravity, the impact of the starfish round as it expanded and tripled in caliber size was enough to knock the can noticeably away from the general. He punched the can twice more as it tumbled away and downward. The faint odor of canned fruit reached him as syrup and fruit cocktail spewed from the holes in the plastic. The booms of the pistol filled ·the corridors, but Spears's hearing was protected by in-canal wolf ears, electronic suppressors that allowed normal sounds in but stopped anything over eighty decibels.

"Good shooting, sir," the unseen marine said.

Spears chuckled. Catshit. A half-blind soldier should be able to hit a target that big at this range. "Use the smaller one next time. Ready . . . throw!"

More booms lapped against the walls as his shots found the next target, a head-sized can of yellow plastic. Spam, it looked like. Now that wasn't bad shooting.

In the Main Assembly area, Powell came to join Wilks and Billie and the others.

"Major?"

"We've got all of Spears's men here except for those he's got with him," Powell said.

"You've lost it, Major," a top kick said. "The general will wipe the floor up with you and your mutineers when he gets back."

"Maybe, Top, but I'll risk that. I'm going to give you all a choice," he said. "Those of you who wish to remain loyal to General Spears and his demented vision, move over to the left there. Those of you who will obey my orders until we can contact SekCom and get an official review of the situation, assemble on the right, by the aft wall."

The docks and ship bays were much larger, but this room was the biggest space normally used for general assemblies. The two hundred or so people rumbled, a disorganized crowd walla, as they spoke to each other and to nobody:

"Powell's lost his fucking mind—"

"I don't wanna wind up feeding the bastards—"

"What's the legal scat here, Sarge—?"

"We're fucked either way—"

"Ah, hell, I'll go with the major—"

Wilks watched as the men, women, and androids chose sides. The bots didn't count, they weren't AI grade; the androids had no choice, really, they were programmed to obey the ranking officer and since Spears was gone, that was Powell. The human group gradually divided into roughly equal numbers moving toward each side of the room. Most of the scientists went with Powell—maybe their exposure to the aliens had taught them something. More enlisted troops went to the aft wall, too, while the line officers, a couple of captains and lieutenants, and most of the NCOs went to the Spears group. That figured. Sergeants mostly ran the day-to-day operations of any military organization and they trusted more in the military process than did the grunts. Officers usually stuck together because they were officers.

"I can't believe so many would still follow him," Powell said softly.

"Hell, I can't believe *you* got so many," Wilks said. "What will we do with them?"

"Put them in detention. It'll be a little crowded but they'll just have to make do."

"What about the crossovers?"

"We'll keep them supervised," Powell said. "Outside of you and a few others, there aren't any of them I would trust with a weapon just yet."

Wilks nodded. "I hear that."

"All right. You men and women on the aft wall, return to your normal stations. You'll be reassigned shortly, keep your coms open, you'll get a computer log telling you where to report. We'll be a little thin but we can keep things running."

Billie said, "What about the general?"

"Yeah," Wilks put in, "do you have any antiskycraft weaponry mounted in the base?"

"Negative," Powell said. "We didn't expect attack from that quarter. Some of the crawlers and hoppers carry light machine guns, 20mm EU slug cannons."

"Enough to bring down a small troop carrier," Wilks said. "Better get somebody you trust who can shoot suited up and into battery, PDQ. The best way to stop Spears is to knock him down before he knows he's in trouble."

"I would prefer to capture him," Powell said.

"With all due respect, Major, as long as Spears is alive he's dangerous. If he gets back here, into the base, he's got an army the same size as yours, plus he's got personal control of the aliens, isn't that right? You said the queens recognize him, didn't you?"

Powell took a deep breath. "That's correct."

"I don't like taking out marines; I've had to do it in the past and I would rather not, but this is what you hired me for, isn't it? The hot work?"

Powell closed his eyes, nodded, resigned. "Yes."

"Fine. You run your base, Major. I'll take care of Spears."

The man nodded again, and Wilks turned away. He wouldn't order anybody to shoot the general but he would stand aside and let Wilks do it. Fine. Whatever it took.

"Come on, Billie. I'd feel better if you stuck with me."

"What about Bueller?"

"He's okay. He's standing by the life-support controls until we're sure what's what."

"Where are we going?"

"To give Spears a welcome home party. Once he's gone, we're gonna put all his pet monsters to sleep."

Billie shook her head. "Thank God."

"Whoever. Let's go."

# 16

"**S**ir, the storm has passed. We can lift whenever you are ready."

Spears nodded, pointed one finger at the trooper in a kind of salute. "Load 'em up."

The men hustled toward the hopper, eager to get out of the place. The air plant belonged to the aliens now, and his human troops were afraid to be here. They didn't have anything to worry about, as long as Spears had a use for them. Soon they would, but not right now. A good general didn't waste matériel until he could see suitable replacement for it on the horizon.

Spears climbed into the trooper carrier and moved to the control cabin. The pilot had all systems online, doubtless had had them ready for some time. Spears grinned. "Lift it," Spears commanded.

The hopper rumbled with power and then surged up a hair, enough to clear the landing area floor. It began to move forward slowly. Once it was clear of the plant, the little ship would become like an arrow shot at a distant target, would hang a lazy parabola, decelerating against the faint gravity for the last portion of the flight. POC—piece of cake.

"I don't hear the beacon," Spears said.

"Probably some residual crosspole flurries, sir. Flux whirlpools causing interference. It's not uncommon after a big storm.

"Is our com working?"

"All systems are green, yes, sir."

"Call Third Base. Coded squirt, advising them of our status."

"Sir."

The pilot slid one finger across a motion-sensitive contact bar, then touched a keypad next to it.

The general watched. Waited.

"There's the response, sir," the pilot said. "Ackno, confirm, green and green."

Spears rubbed at his chin with his thumb. Missed a spot with the depil last time he'd wiped the whiskers off. Just a couple of hairs, but that was sloppy. Sloppy was bad. Sloppy could get you dead.

"Call 'em back. Punch in code 096-9011-D, that's delta."

"Sir? I don't recognize the code—"

"You aren't supposed to, son. Just do what you're told."

"Yessir."

The pilot tapped in the numbers.

The hopper had full holoprojics. After a moment
the screen area over the console blossomed,
swirled for a moment, then remained a pale and
featureless blue. A clear signal.

"Well, well," Spears said. "We've got trouble at
home."

"Sir? There's nothing there."

"Exactly."

The pilot looked puzzled. Spears said, "You don't
know the story of the barking dog, do you, son?"

The pilot shook his head.

"Back on Earth, long time ago, there was a famous investigator working on a crime. While listing
the clues, he said, 'And of course, there's the matter of the dog barking in the night.' His assistant,
who had been compiling the evidence, said, 'But
the dog did not bark.' 'Precisely,' the detective
said."

The pilot might as well have been in suspended
animation, midpoint in a fifty-year sleep. Spears
shook his head. "The signal is not supposed to be
clear," the general said. "That it is means there is
a problem."

"Ah. I see."

Whether he did or not didn't matter. Spears was
not so inept that he would leave his base without
stringing a few noisemakers. Time to try another
one. There was always a chance that the magnetic
storm had damaged some electronics.

"Put the ship back down where it was," Spears
said.

"Sir?"

"A little detour. Don't worry about it."

                    •   •   •

Wilks pushed the helmet back on the E-suit. The heaters in the crawler had the somewhat stale air warm enough to breathe and keep his ears from freezing. Billie sat in the co-operator's chair, waiting for him to tell her what he wanted.

"Okay, we have to assume that his hopper has got firepower equal to ours, so we have to shoot first. The weaponry here is like that on the APC we flew on the aliens' homeworld. Robot guns, computer-operated, 20mm expended uranium armor-piercing slugs. All we have to do is plug the target in, like so . . ." He tapped in the specs for a light military hopper. "Light the system, here . . ." He lifted a protective cover, pressed a button. The fire control screen flicked on. "Security code, courtesy of Major Powell, thus . . ." The screen flashed. ARMED, it said. SYSTEM READY.

"That's it. Everything is automatic from here on. The ship gets into range, our system hoses it."

"He's got twenty-five troopers with him," Billie said. "You ever hear the expression 'burning down the barn to get rid of the rats'?"

"Depends on how nasty the rats are, kid. The guys with him are on his side. You can't think about them or their families or anything like that."

"That's cold, Wilks."

"War is ugly, Billie. People die. Sometimes the choice comes down to you or them. If Spears gets back here and rallies the troops who might be loyal to him, the rest of us are going to wind up feeding mama bug and the little ones. In a perfect universe there wouldn't be any need for soldiers or marines. In this one, there is."

Billie nodded, despite her feelings. He was right,

she knew it. She had killed before, both APs and humans. She remembered the pirate who had attacked their ship, and how he would have blown them all out of existence. She didn't like it, but Wilks was right.

"But if the guns are automatic, why do we have to be here?"

He shrugged. "Like a pilot on a commercial arc ship. In case something goes wrong. A circuit could overload, something could jam, maybe the guns work fine but somebody gets clear of the hopper in an escape pod and keeps coming. We're backup."

Billie repressed a sigh. Humans, backing a death-dealing machine. She sometimes wondered if people were any better than the aliens. They were killers, but more like ants or bees. Beast of prey, they hunted to feed, not for sport. And she doubted if they ever planned an ambush of their own kind.

Then again, Billie had no desire to become dinner for the monsters. She had come too close too many times already. And people like Spears, like those turncoats on Earth who caught and gave their fellow humans to the aliens, those kind of people were psychotic. Whatever it took to stop them had to be done. She just wished she wasn't the one who had to do it.

"General? The hopper is ten klicks out."

Spears, looking at a computer read, turned toward the pilot. "Keep it on standard approach."

"Sir."

The hopper in which they rode smelled musty, the air stale, and while everything worked as it was supposed to work, the little ship felt loggy. Spears could understand that; the backup vessel had been in storage at the air plant for more than a year, parked and sealed, awaiting just such a use as this. The hopper on which they had flown from the base was five kilometers ahead of them now, empty of personnel, being piloted on remote by the man who normally would be flying this vessel. The copilot seated next to him kept the chase hopper on an even path, same altitude, same speed. Not that it was really necessary—*this* ship had a major advantage over the drone ahead of them; this ship wore a full stealth suit, would be invisible to radar or Doppler, and with the flat-black anodized hull damned near invisible to eyeballing against the dark of space. Still, if the hide-me suit somehow malfunctioned, a lazy radar operator would see a double blip and probably think it was a ghost. Since there weren't supposed to be any other hoppers the same size away from the base—this one didn't show on records anywhere, Spears had seen to that—then the operator who *might* see it, *if* the stealth gear failed, would not be unduly worried. And if, in this very unlikely scenario, the tech didn't scramble a code, he would be fed to the aliens when Spears got back. The general had no use for such troops, even if he was the one trying to fool them.

"Five klicks, sir."

"Steady as she goes, son." This could all be a waste of his trump, but Spears had learned it was better to be cautious than dead. Time was running down on this planetoid anyway. There were big things in the offing, worlds to conquer, glory to be reaped. Wars to be won.

Spears grinned. And victory begins at home, doesn't it?

"Here they come," Wilks said. "Right down the pipe."

The tiny green dot on the gunnery radar screen moved toward the center. After a moment, the dot began to pulse, alternating now between green and amber.

TARGET INITIALLY ACQUIRED, flashed across the bottom of the screen.

"It's a match," Wilks said.

The alternating dot continued to pulse, then went from green/amber to red.

TARGET CONFIRMED. TO ABORT FIRING YOU MUST ENTER CANCEL CODE.

Wilks glanced at Billie. Shook his head. "All yours," he said, knowing that the computer wouldn't understand the comment.

The pulsing dot expanded, became the outline of the hopper. A blue grid appeared on the screen in one corner, then expanded to cover the hopper. A bull's-eye ring lit in bright green, centered on the hopper.

SIXTY SECONDS TO OPTIMUM FIRING DISTANCE.

A timer began counting down from sixty toward zero.

Wilks watched Billie. She stared at the screen, blinked rapidly. Her breathing speeded up. At fire minus thirty seconds, she said, "Jesus, it's like watching an execution."

"Yeah, it is."

FIFTEEN SECONDS TO OPTIMUM FIRING DISTANCE.

Wilks tapped a control on the external monitor.

The tracking cam gave him a star-sprinkled black. "There it is," he said, as much to himself as Billie. A tiny dot, the running lights barely visible.

FIVE SECONDS TO OPTIMUM FIRING DISTANCE.

The hydraulics of the guns whined slightly as they moved the weapons, tracking the incoming ship.

OPTIMUM FIRING DISTANCE. COMMENCE FIRING.

The machine guns were recoilless so the vessel around them didn't shudder, but the weapons vibrated, shaking them as if they had developed a sudden palsy. And the vacuum outside didn't carry any sound, but some of the hull and air inside did. The reports were muted by the dampers, the noise almost like a thick sheet of canvas being ripped. Every tenth round was a tracer, and the guns fired so rapidly that there seemed to be a continuous line of colorful fire splashing against the incoming hopper. The fire computer had it all figured out: the target's speed, the gravity, the velocity of the incredibly hard uranium slugs that hammered the hopper. It couldn't miss.

It didn't miss.

The hopper's armor wasn't enough. The machine-gun fire punched through it. Wilks could see sparks as bullets hit the plating, sparks that blossomed as air from within spewed out and fed the tiny fires.

The tracers raked the ship, found the engine, smashed through and destroyed it. The hopper lost power, tumbled, out of control. Fell in the low gravity, a ruined and discarded toy from the hand of a bored child.

"God," Billie said.

Wilks watched. No escape pods popped out. It was almost too easy. See you in hell, Spears.

"Sir, the drone is drawing fire!"

Spears nodded, pleased. "Set your fire control to backwalk the attacking battery."

"We'll have to drop the stealth suit to use our targeting systems."

"That doesn't matter. We've got the drop on them. Punch them out."

The pilot and copilot hurried to obey.

Got to be Powell behind this, Spears thought. I wouldn't have guessed that you had the guts, you little no-dick bastard. But if you want to play with the best, you have got to be a lot sharper than a chickenshit ambush, Major. I am going to hand-feed you to the queen myself when I get down.

The hopper went down, streaming oxy-fed flames that winked out quickly in the vac. The ship hit, bounced high, hit again, shattered, and sent pieces flying. The light gravity let most of the debris sail quite a distance. Those chunks that entered the station's faux grav fell faster, bounced lower. The tracking cam stayed with the largest section. Wilks didn't see any bodies but he supposed they were all cocooned into their seats. Just as well. The sight of a ruined human body tumbling across the landscape wasn't one he particularly wanted to see anyhow.

Adios, General.

SECOND TARGET ACQUIRED, the computer flashed. OPTIMUM DISTANCE MINUS ONE THOUSAND METERS. COMMENCING FIRE.

Wilks jumped. Stared at the screen. It took a second to register, a second they didn't have to spare.

"Fuck! Close your helmet! Move! We've got to get out of here, now!"

He slapped his own faceplate shut, grabbed Billie's hand, and jerked her up. They scrambled for the exit. He hit the emergency hatch control, both locks snapped up.

They leapt for the opening as the first slugs began to punch holes in the crawler.

# 17

$S$pears watched the hard metal teeth of his machine guns chew the crawler to pieces. He felt a certain satisfaction in knowing he had outsmarted his enemy, had not fallen into the trap. Had not been outsmarted.

The crawler shuddered under the impact, vibrating, shaking. They were close enough so the combat belly cam picked up the two troopers abandoning the landcraft, running away from the doomed vessel.

"Cut them down," Spears said. If he'd thought about it longer, he might not have given that order, the new troops always needed unspoiled containers and food, but once an order was given, he was not a man to belay it unless he had good reason. Canceling orders given in the midst of combat reflected badly on a commander; it made him look indecisive. Nor did it matter that these men wouldn't be around to remember these orders much longer— Spears was not an indecisive man.

The crawler continued its bullet-driven dance, and the two troopers kept sprinting. "Was I unclear in my speech?" Spears said, his voice cool and tight.

"N-no, sir. But the computer is locked on the crawler. I'll have to reset it for human targets."

"Do so."

"Sir."

The pilot's hands fluttered. The machine guns whined on their hydraulic gyros, began to alter their aim.

Too late. The fleeing pair achieved the safety of the station, disappearing from view.

"Sorry, sir."

"Never mind. The crawler is dead, that was the primary threat. Hose down the other craft on the apron."

"Sir—?"

"Destroy them. We don't want to get shot in the back and we do want the only operating vehicles out here."

The pilot nodded. "Yes, sir."

One of the rules of combat was to do your enemy enough damage so he couldn't recover in time to damage you. Spears had control of the airspace and he intended to keep it. And while Powell might think he had the station buttoned up, there were ways inside that he didn't know about. A wise officer never let himself be caught without an entrance or an exit. Powell was not wise. Spears was.

• • •

Billie's breath came hard, the suit's tanks hadn't been designed to supply so much oxygen so quickly. But they were inside, and safe. For now.

Wilks was already halfway out of his climate suit, rushing toward a com mounted on the lock wall. He slapped the com.

"This is Wilks. We've got a fubar here, Powell. Spears sent in a decoy hopper. He's taken out our crawler, we're in the South Lock. Billie, what's going on out there?"

Billie moved to the lock, triggered the observation cam next to it. The little holoproj lit up. Dust puffed up in little spurts around the various vessels sitting on the ground. An occasional spark glittered on the craft, and as she watched, one of the hoppers canted wildly to one side, the support struts suddenly collapsed.

Billie turned back toward Wilks. "They're shooting up all the hoppers and crawlers," she said.

"You get that?" Wilks said into the com.

Powell's voice when it came through the speaker was nervous: "God. What are we going to do? He could peel open the station like a banana!"

"He won't," Wilks said. "He doesn't want to risk damaging the aliens. But he'll have an attack plan figured out. We underestimated him. If he knew enough to give us a decoy to shoot at, he'll know a way in we aren't expecting. Get whatever troops you can trust with weapons armed, fast, get a combat opchan working and cover every lock. And get anybody who might be loyal to Spears into a secured area PDQ."

Powell said, "That won't be easy, we can't be sure—"

"Listen, Major, we damn well *can* be sure that if somebody opens a door and lets Spears in we will be in very deep shit. Don't take any chances. If there is any doubt about a trooper's loyalty to you, put him behind a thick door."

"All right. I understand."

"I'll meet you in Command Center in five minutes."

Wilks turned to Billie. "The general is knocking out our ability to fight him in the air, or escape on the surface. He'll be occupied with that for a while. Come on."

"Where are we going?"

"Powell can issue the orders but he isn't a combat soldier. He is going to need somebody he can trust telling him what to do. I fucked up once, we can't afford to let that happen again."

"How bad is it?" she asked.

"It could be worse. We've got the high ground. Spears can spend all his troops at one spot and we've got to cover every entrance, so we'll be thin, but he's got to come in through a lock and we can watch all of them. As long as it's our troops on the doors, we should be able to keep him out. Powell will be scrambling the entrance codes and putting the station on full alert, soon as he gets the general's men dogged down. Odds are still in our favor, though I should have had Powell set this all up before we tried to pot Spears. I thought sure we could knock him down. I guess that's why he's a general and I'm a sergeant. Come on."

They ran.

·   ·   ·   ·

"Status?" Spears said. His blood was up, he felt like a hunter tracking dangerous prey. There was some risk, to be sure, but no doubt that he would win in the end. Whatever the cost.

"Sir, all of the exterior landcraft and aircraft have been immobilized. All engines appear to be dysfunctional, power mains knocked out."

Spears nodded. "Good." Of course, there were the starships inside the base, but nobody was going to use those for flitting around on the planetoid's surface. And if Powell planned to run in the star transports, he had a big surprise coming. Spears had never bothered locking the crawlers and hoppers into his personal keycode—there wasn't anywhere to run *to* on the planetoid—but the offworld vessels wouldn't lift a centimeter unless he okayed it. No, Powell and his little band of insurrectionists weren't going anywhere. They were bottled up in the station and while they might think they had the edge, they were also mistaken about that.

"Put us down at these coordinates," Spears said. He rattled off the grid numbers. Without asking why, the pilot obeyed. There was a blind spot just east of the North Lock, a corridor not much wider than twenty meters that led right to the fusion plant's heat sinks. The big aluminum and ceramic plates could be used to radiate excess warmth away from the station, did there happen to be an overload the environmental pipes couldn't handle. A careful platoon could march along that no-cam corridor to the sinks, then duck the security scanners and go in either direction. Nobody would see them approach a lock; nobody would know company was coming until they knocked on the door.

True, the doors would all be scramble-secured and guarded, if Powell had any brains at all, but Spears had an answer for that.

Another big surprise for the mutineers.

No, there wasn't any doubt as to the victory. The main thing now was to do it clean, by the numbers. A hundred years from now they would be teaching tactics based on scenarios that Spears created. Might as well begin dazzling the future now.

Powell looked as if he were about to try to climb a wall, Billie thought, watching the man pace. His hands shook, he was pale, sweat beaded at his hairline and on his upper lip. There were a dozen carbines side by side on a table in the room, with boxes of magazines stacked next to them. While Wilks went to talk to Powell, Billie moved toward the weapons. Whatever happened, she wasn't going to be standing by helplessly.

A trooper with a carbine slung across his chest and held ready started to swing his weapon around as Billie approached.

"Wilks," Billie said.

Wilks turned away from Powell. "Let her have one," he said to the trooper.

The man didn't even glance at Powell for confirmation. He knew who was in charge, whatever the ranks involved. He nodded.

Billie picked up a carbine, racked the action, checked it over—the gun was empty—then pulled a magazine from an open box and loaded it into the piece. She took three more hundred-round AP mags from the box and put them into her pockets, one under her belt. With four hundred shots, she could theoretically kill a whole lot of things, if they didn't get her first. She slung the weapon over her shoulder. She felt a little better, now that she was armed.

Wilks and Powell went back and forth; it was easy to see that Powell was scared shitless. He was a man of peace, Wilks had told her, should have been a preacher or a medic and not a soldier. Civilized men didn't make very good warriors.

Billie moved to a wall-mounted com. Told the routing computer to connect her with Mitch.

"Bueller here."

There was no visual, Billie didn't know if that was on purpose or not, but he obviously couldn't see her.

"Mitch," she said.

"Billie. You okay?"

"I'm with Wilks in the Command Center," she said. "We're fine."

"I saw you escape from the crawler," he said. "I was worried about you."

"No problem. What are you doing there?"

"I'm going to stay in Environment Control until we are certain of a stable situation. If Spears or his troops get inside, I might be able to do some good here, shut down air or heating or lights and slow them up some. I wouldn't do much good on the line."

Billie nodded, realized he couldn't see that, said, "I understand." And she did. Wilks had told her that the APs designed for the run to the aliens' homeworld were crack marines, able to outshoot, outrun, and outfight ordinary men in virtually every combat scenario. The problem was that Mitch's conditioning, Asimov's Modified Laws, wouldn't allow him to kill humans. Unless he was certain a wound wouldn't do that, he couldn't shoot a man, even though he could put a bullet into one virtually anywhere he chose at combat ranges. A man might bleed to death from a shattered foot, after all, and androids weren't allowed to risk that. Except, of course, for those who had been built without the Laws inculcated into them. Which was supposed to be impossible, though Billie knew better. Most of the pirates who'd attacked them on that fucked-up mission had been such androids, able to kill.

"Listen, Mitch, when this is all over, we need to sit down and talk. I haven't been treating you very well, I don't understand everything about it, but I want to do better."

"Thank you, Billie. You don't know how glad I am to hear that."

"No guarantees," she said. "I mean, I don't know what exactly is going to come of it."

"Anything is better than nothing," he said.

She felt uncomfortable. She was still pissed at him, but the idea of dying or of his dying didn't feel good. Not at all. "Okay, listen, I've got to discom. I'll talk to you later."

"You be very careful," he said. "I don't want anything to happen to you. I—I—"

"Don't say it, Mitch. Not yet."

She shut the com down.

Behind her, Wilks and Powell had begun yelling at each other.

"Listen," Wilks said, his voice hard, "get the fucking locks covered! Weld them shut, especially the cargo doors! You don't know what kind of code-breaking gear Spears might have. He might have access to the mainframe from out there."

"Impossible, the system is shielded, the internal modems are hardened—"

"Dammit, Powell, this man is a soldier, career military, and he suckered us once. If he gets inside and starts blasting, a lot of people are going to die. You didn't know about the second hopper, did you?"

Powell's jaw was set tight, his lips thinned and white, but he shook his head. "No."

"You can tape it that he's got something else up his sleeve. We're self-sufficient here, all he's got outside is field rations and gear. If we can keep him outside long enough, we win."

Powell blew out a short breath. "All right. I'll give the order."

Wilks nodded. Looked at Billie. Billie didn't know much about military matters, but it seemed as if the next move was up to Spears. She didn't like that very much. The man was crazy. There was no telling what he was going to do. All they could do was wait.

In his C-suit, Spears led his platoon along the wall under the sinks toward the East Lock. The traitors would have lost the hopper when it veered north and would probably be expecting an attack from that quarter. True, they probably could have gone in at the North Lock as easily as the East, once the fifth column struck, but Spears was thinking about posterity now. If he could finish this without losing too many of his troops, it would look better to one viewing historical tapes. What an amazing commander, they would say. How adept.

Spears nodded to himself as he reached the hiding spot next to the East Lock. Nobody knew they were here. He had his demolitions expert set the explosive charges on the lock door itself, stressing great care, using only hand signals and helmet-to-helmet conduction, all radios were off.

The charges set, his men in readiness, Powell pulled the special transmitter from his tool belt and looked at the covered button. He had not expected it would ever really come to this, but no man would ever be able to say that General Thomas A.W. Spears had been caught with his pants down in this combatsit.

He flipped the button cover up with his gloved thumb and pressed the control once, hard. Grinned behind his faceplate. Powell and his little band of would-be heroes were about to have something to worry about in there.

Yes, sir, right now, the security door to the queen's chamber would be sliding up, along with the protective covers holding twenty-five of the drones captive.

And a tiny holographic image of Spears would be standing behind the queen, waving a torch in his hand, urging her out of her chamber.

Spears chuckled, imagining the queen's surprise. And Powell's surprise, too.

"Dinnertime," Spears said. "Come and get it."

# 18

"**M**otherfucker!" a man screamed. Gunfire rattled.

In the CC, Wilks said, "Powell—?"

"It's the guard at the queen's chamber," Powell said, touching controls on the monitor. The picture splashed into life in full color, the holoproj of the security cam revealing the guard firing his weapon at something offscreen.

Powell fiddled with the controls; the view shifted slightly. Revealed the open door.

"Oh, man!" Wilks said.

The guard screamed again. The man who had been so nasty to Wilks and Billie when they'd gone to see the chamber.

A spiked tail shot into sight, impaled the screaming trooper, punched through his chest as easily as a needle pierces thin cloth. The man went slack, his weapon falling. The massive ridged tail snapped like a whip and the man flew out of the frame.

"Sweet baby Jesus," Powell said.

"He's turned the queen loose," Wilks said. "Spears."

Other reports began flooding in over the op-chan.

The queen had company.

"Get to the starships," Wilks said, his face grim. "This base is contaminated. We're all dead if we stay here." But at least the son of a bitch's plan was also shot. He'd play hell rounding up the monsters with the men he had left.

Five minutes after the queen and her brood were set free and encouraged to kill anything in their way, Spears nodded, and the demolitions man blew the hatch. The shaped charge was silent in the absence of air, but the metal of the lock peeled open and the oxy inside spewed out, freezing into powdery white crystals in the cold night.

"Go!"

Guards inside began firing, the ones who hadn't been knocked sprawling by the concussion, at least. Spears's men had the advantage of surprise, however, and only one of his troops went down before the lock was secured. They were in, the enemy was in disarray, and this mission was going as well as anybody could expect. All the feeds from his men were going into the hopper's recorder. He would edit them later, for the sake of continuity, of course. He would look heroic enough; after all, he wasn't an armchair commander, and the record would show him right in the thick of things.

And he wasn't done yet, oh, no. Those who had crossed him would regret it, assuming they lived long enough for that thought.

Inside the inner lock, he motioned for his troops to open their faceplates. "Let's move," he said. "Keep your suits patent, they'll probably try to mess with life support. Go to opchan six, scrambled. No point in radio silence now they know we're here." With that, he snapped his own faceplate shut. "Try to keep some of them alive," he said. "Shoot low."

Wilks ran, carbine held ready to fire, Billie and Powell right behind him. The station's battle alarm screeched, a high-low *wee-wanh* that repeated itself over and over. Red lights flashed at every turning of the hallway, and men and women ran in panic, fleeing something most of them knew about but hadn't encountered yet.

Most of the ones who'd encountered the aliens would likely be unable to flee, Wilks knew. Spears had let the goddamned things out, somehow, and they would be in a feeding frenzy, collecting every human they could get their claws on, given what he knew about them.

Billie had found a portable com and was using it.

"Mitch! Mitch, answer me! Get out of there, meet us at the ship bay! The aliens are loose! Spears is in the station! Mitch!"

If Bueller heard her, he wasn't responding. Wilks didn't have time to worry about it at the moment.

An alien lurched out into the hallway from an open door, turned toward the three of them, and opened those hellish jaws. Slime dripped from the teeth in long strings.

"Fuck you," Wilks said. He popped the carbine up, found the manual front sight—no time to mess with the laser—and fired a quick burst.

The armor-piercing rounds smashed the alien's face, shards of its hard chitin flew, acid sprayed. It fell sideways and backward, hit the wall, slid to the floor.

The blast of the caseless rounds hit Wilks's ears like a flat slap from a heavy hand. His ears rang. Damn. Should have put his plugs in. Oh, well. If he lived long enough to worry about growing deaf in his old age, he could deal with that.

The liquid on the floor bubbled and sent up clouds of stinking smoke as it ate through the treadplate.

"Watch the blood, don't step in it!"

They ran.


A trooper came around the corner with his weapon up. Spears was the first one to see him. He drew his pistol, brought it up and smacked his gun-hand into the waiting palm of his other hand, hit a classic isosceles stance and fired three times. The technique was called the Mozambique Double Tap, the name having to do with some ancient police action in some African country before space travel. It was a standard pistol procedure: two in the heart, one in the head, always in that order. Spears guessed that it dated from a time when body armor was sometimes hidden under regular clothing and to make certain of a kill, a backup shot was taken at an unprotected target.

The unfortunate trooper wasn't wearing armor,

so any of the three shots would have been sufficient to kill him.

As the man fell, Spears felt that sense of
triumph, that rush of *survival* he always got whenever he killed somebody one-on-one. It brought
back old memories. All the way from when he'd
been a boy and had taken out his first opponent
ever—

Tommy hid in the supply closet, among the
brooms and vacuum cleaners and fragrant tubs of
cleaneze. The granular cleaning compound made
his nose itch, made him want to sneeze, but he
pinched his nostrils shut so he wouldn't.

Outside the dark closet, Jerico Axe prowled the
dim hall, looking for Tommy. It was past quench-
light, everybody was supposed to be asleep, the
adult marines and medicos would be in bed by
now, but not Jerico.

Jerico was a stupid asshole, Tommy knew, but he
was a big stupid asshole and he was mean. Tommy
had gotten on Jerico's shit list, he didn't know how,
and now every time the bastard saw him out of an
adult's sight, he would proceed to kick Tommy's
ass. Not that Tommy didn't fight back, he did, but
Jerico had been decanted first, he was older, ten
kilos heavier, and six months ahead of Tommy in
martial arts skills. Tommy got in a few licks now
and then, he'd broken the cocksucker's nose once,
but that had cost a broken arm of his own, plus two
teeth had to be reimplanted and fifteen staples
over his left eye.

What Tommy wished was that Jerico would take
a hike along the Deep Rim and trip, bouncing all

the way to the bottom where he'd rot in the hot sun and not be found until the carrion birds were finished with him.

Might as well wish for a commission while you're at it, dickhead, he told himself. Jerico wasn't that stupid.

Tommy sat in the closet, hoping Jerico wouldn't think to look for him in here. He was tired, he wanted to go to bed, to get some rest before drill at dawn, but here he was having to hide to keep from getting pounded.

Bare feet slapped the floor outside the closet. Jerico had taken his boots off, but he still lumbered like a broken robot, making plenty of noise. Tommy heard the bathroom door creak as the thug went to look for him in there.

Shit. He would look in here, too. There was no real place to hide, unless he wanted to climb into the cleaneze bag mounted on the roller bin. Sure, if he dug down through the dirty cleaner, crouched real low and buried himself in it, Jerico wouldn't see him.

Tommy stood, started to put one leg over the rim of the bag, then stopped. Abruptly a rage filled him, a hot anger that bubbled up through his legs and groin, flooded into his chest, swirled fluidly into his skull.

*Fuck this!*

It wasn't right! He shouldn't have to hide from dicklick Jerico Axe, just because he was bigger and stronger and better trained than Tommy. It wasn't right.

With only the glows coming from the instrument panels of the cleaning bot parked next to the door,

the room was dark, but there was just enough light
for Tommy to see the baseboard scraper mounted
in the bot's accessory rack. It was a little over half
a meter long, an aluminum rod nearly as thick as
Tommy's wrist, connected to a dull blade set at an
angle. The bot used the tool to clean the grit from
the baseboards, it looked kind of like a garden hoe
somebody had bent crooked.

Tommy peeled the scraper from the bot's rack.
Hefted it. It was fairly heavy.

When Jerico opened the door, Tommy was ready.

The larger boy had time to blink, his eyes going
wide, as Tommy jumped and buried the blunt corner of the blade in Jerico's skull. Hit him just over
the right eye. It made a satisfying *chunk!*

Jerico screamed—that was nice, too—and stumbled backward across the hall until his back
smacked into the far wall. He slid down, tugged the
scraper from his head, moaned as the blood poured
into his eye. He looked up at Tommy, stunned, as if
he couldn't understand what had happened.

Tommy moved toward Jerico. "Here, gimme
that," he said. He grabbed the scraper. Jerico let it
go. What he thought, Tommy didn't know, but the
fear he had felt, the shame of being afraid, his
rage, all combined into something he'd never felt
before. He felt a great strength now, a power, at
having defeated his enemy.

"I'm bleeding!"

"Not for long," Tommy said.

He raised the scraper again and moved in.

Tommy Spears was nine years old the night he
killed his first enemy—

•   •   •   •

"Holy shit!" one of Spears's marines yelled.

The general snapped out of his memory fugue and looked past the fallen soldier. Amazing. The entire memory had flashed past, maybe five seconds in realtime, all jammed and compressed like a squeezed data file on a modem squirt.

One of the alien drones stood there, readying itself to attack.

Spears stepped forward so an overhead light shone directly down on his face. Saw the alien see him.

"You know who I am," he said. He pulled a control from his belt. "And the queen knows what this is." He waved the transmitter. The floor of the egg room was wired with explosives and this control would set them off. Spears had made sure the queen knew that. Of course, by now, she would have her drones hauling the eggs out, hoping to find a safer place for them, but she wouldn't have had time to move them all yet, and besides *that*, she couldn't know if Spears had wired the whole fucking station so he could blow it all into orbit.

What the drones saw, the queen knew.

The drone hissed, then turned and ran the opposite way.

"Holy shit," the trooper said again. "It was *scared* of you!"

"Damn straight," Spears said. "With good reason. Let's go."

The platoon never hesitated.


"Powell?"

"This way," the major said.

Wilks turned to look at her. "I'm fine," Billie said, though she was out of breath. "But Mitch—"

"—tastes bad," Wilks said. "If he stands still, they'll walk right past him."

"Spears won't," Powell said.

"Thank you, Major." To Billie, he said, "Look, he knows where we're going, he'll do what he can to make sure we make it and then he'll be along."

"I can't leave him here," Billie said.

"Fine. We'll wait for him. I promise."

Billie nodded. It would have to do. She didn't have a lot of choice. She would have to trust Wilks.

Somebody screamed behind them, a sound that trailed off into a liquid gurgle.

"The clock is running, folks."

It seemed to Billie that she had been running most of her life. This was not the time nor the place to stop and take stock. "Go," she said. "I'm right behind you."

They went.

# 19

Wilks was not afraid to die. He ran toward what he considered the safest place on this tiny planet, but if he didn't make it, well, too bad. He'd been living on borrowed time since his first meeting with the aliens, so long ago. What had it been? Twelve, fourteen standard years? Billie had been ten, he'd have to ask her how old she was now. He should have died with his squad then, but he hadn't, and he'd spent a great deal of drink and chem trying to forget it. Fate hadn't wanted that, the powers-that-be in the universe, not to mention the Colonial Marines, had thrown it all back into his face. Somewhere along the way he had come up with a new purpose: to wipe the aliens out, down to the last drone, the last egg. Getting himself killed here would prevent him from accomplishing his mission, and *that* bothered him more than dying. Once in his life there had been personal fear, but those days were long gone.

A few years back during one of his two-week chem binges, Wilks had been picked up in an alley by civilians. He was naked and his ID implants had been fuzzed by the people who'd robbed and then tried to kill him, to keep the authorities from identifying the body. Not knowing he was military, the civilians had stuck him into a medicenter and given him the standard life-support treatment, which included sessions with psychiatric types. It had been a teaching hospital and there were plenty of young medics eager to work with such an obviously depressed patient; surely that unrevised scar on his face bespoke worlds of mental impairment?

It didn't take long for them to peg him as a career marine and diagnose his problem. But while waiting for the medical MPs to come and fetch him, they hustled to get as many budding headbenders as they could exposed to him. Chances like this didn't come along very often.

In one of these sessions, with an attractive young woman he would have tried to bed under other circumstances, he first heard about the Doc Holliday Syndrome.

Holliday, it seemed, had been some kind of medical man in the Terran frontier times, a dentist or some such. He developed a fatal and, at the time, incurable illness.

"So," the young doctor said, "he packed up, moved to a drier climate, which was supposed to offer some symptomatic comfort for his remaining days, and became a professional gambler and outlaw. He engaged in a number of gunfights, and although he wasn't a particularly adept shooter, always managed to prevail over his opponents. There is an instance, for example, where M. Holliday fired upon a man inside a public drinking establishment using a period weapon called a six-shooter. He was within seven meters of his opponent, emptied his weapon, and missed entirely. Given that the six-shooter was supposedly accurate to a range of fifty meters in the hand of an expert, this was considered poor marksmanship. He later switched to a weapon called a shotgun, which, I am informed, is dangerous over a somewhat wider area."

"How interesting," Wilks told the young shrink. Maybe he *would* try to fuck her, if for no other reason than to shut her up.

Before he could speak, however, she continued, obviously in love with the sound of her own voice. "From what our medico-historical researchers can determine, the primary reason Holliday won his duels was because he did not care if he did."

That brought a frown to Wilks's face. "What does that mean?" He was immediately sorry he had asked.

"M. Holliday was going to die soon, or so he thought. Actually he lived well beyond his predicted termination, the diagnosis having been somewhat erroneous. But because he *thought* his days were numbered and that this number was very small, he believed he had nothing to lose. Whenever he faced somebody in a duel—they called them shootdowns or showdowns or some such testosteronic euphemistic nonsense—he had no fear of dying. He was, in his own mind, already dead. Further, he regularly imbibed large amounts of alcoholic beverages and was thus further anesthetized. While this doubtless impaired his physical responses vis-à-vis his reaction time and weapons' prowess, these things in fact gave him a psychological edge. Most of the people he faced in such duels did *not* wish to die and thus their fear often caused them to hesitate or behave in a panicky manner. Against an opponent who sincerely did not care if he lived or died but whose only goal was to shoot them and be damned, such fears can be fatal. And apparently these encounters were fatal more often than not against M. Holliday, D.D.S."

Wilks shook his head. He wondered if she talked like that when she came. "Wonderful. You want to take off your clothes and screw a war hero before they come to get me?"

The young woman smiled, unfazed by his crude invitation. "I think not, Corporal Wilks. It would hardly be professional . . ."

Running down a corridor with alien monsters searching for him, Wilks grinned, the scar on his face doubtless making the expression hideous to see. I know just how you felt, Doc. When you live on borrowed time and don't give a dog's dick if you die, it makes things nice and simple.

Billie saw a man holding a carbine squatting behind a bulkhead extrusion, trying to hide. When he saw her spot him, he started to point his weapon at them.

"Wilks!" she yelled. She brought her own carbine around to cover the trooper.

"Don't do it, marine!" Powell called out.

But the trooper was rising, still swinging his piece toward them. "The general is back! You're all dead meat!"

Billie and Wilks fired at about the same time. The trooper did a twisting jig as he fell, his chest blown open, his blood splattering the wall.

Billie felt sick. Killing people never got any easier. But she kept moving. Self-preservation ruled.

Somebody had killed the lights and life support in the corridor but Spears was prepared for that. His troops were suited, in full combat gear. "Go to spookeyes, marines," he ordered. He clicked his own faceplate filters into Amplite mode, saw the corridor light up a ghostly green. Another control flicked on his lamps and the glow that would look a dim and almost invisible violet to unaided eyes splashed the walls with brilliant green, almost as bright as the normal overheads. "Stay sharp, troops! Overlapping fields of fire!"

Somebody stumbled into view twenty meters ahead. Spears saw the man waving his arms, heard him call out: "General! Is that you? Don't shoot, I'm on your side!" He couldn't see much, Spears could tell that, he wore station coveralls, didn't have a weapon or vision augmenters.

"Fire," Spears commanded.

The two marines running point opened up. The sounds were muted but audible. The man ahead fell as if his legs had disappeared. Many inside the station would be his allies but Spears couldn't take time now to worry about loyalties. One enemy with a grenade could cause a lot of damage. Better to clear the halls first and sort things out later.

Abruptly the gravity shut off. There was no warning, merely a sudden cessation. The running marines bounded high into the air, slammed into the walls or ceiling, or tumbled along the floor, out of control. Switching from nearly a full gee to a tenth or less between steps was not something a man could realistically train for.

"Switch on your boots!" Spears yelled.

There were magnetic strips under the floors, put there for just such a failure, and the combat boots would allow walking, albeit a much slower pace than in normal gravity.

When the confusion settled down, along with the troopers, only one man had been injured too badly to continue. The platoon medic said he'd broken his neck and would need full rehab.

"Can he move?"

"No, sir. He's paralyzed."

"Leave him, then. Somebody will come for him later."

Some *thing*, actually, Spears figured. The man was useless as a soldier now, save as fodder for the new troops. Might as well let them have him.

"Sir!" the wounded man cried out. "Please. Don't leave me here for those things!"

"They also serve who lie and wait," Spears said. "It's war, son. You fucked up, you pay for it. Let's move, troops."

They shuffled along, boots clumping on the deck. The cries of the injured man stopped when Spears had his unit switch radio freaks to opchan three.

Powell listened to the com he carried, shook his head. He and Billie and Wilks were in the ap-

proach corridor leading to the starship hangars.
They still had lights and power, though much of
the station had apparently been shut down. Panicky reports came over the com, voices blending
into a continuous and frightened walla:

"Life support shut down in D-2—!"

"It got Maury, it just took him—!"

"Air doors are down, air doors down—!"

"—are under fire, somebody is shooting here—!"

"Monsters, monsters—ahh, get away—!"

The sound of explosions, gunfire, metal on
metal, and other sounds of death and confusion
came, too.

For a moment Wilks felt himself grow heavier, as
if somebody had suddenly put a weight on his back.
Then the feeling vanished.

"Wilks?"

"Somebody is fiddling with the gravity," he said.
"Bueller, trying to slow Spears down, or throw the
aliens off stride, probably."

Powell was on the edge of full-blown panic himself, Wilks could see that. His face was pale, sweaty,
and he clutched at the com as if it were some kind
of lifeline. "The base is overrun," he said. "We're
fucked. I should have known better than to try
Spears. He's a killer. He's a madman. We're all
doomed."

"Listen," Wilks said, as if talking to a buzzhead
recruit or a small child. "Listen, we can get away.
We'll take one of the starships."

Powell shook his head. "Can't. It takes too long to
program a launch. They'll get us. They'll get us."

"We'll run an old program," Wilks said. "Take
one of the ships back to where it came from."

"Not a good idea. They came from Earth. All of them."

"We'll fix the goddamned program along the way! Move, Powell!"

Powell stared at him. Nodded. "Okay. You're in charge now, okay?"

Poor sucker. He should have gone into another line of work. Powell should be drinking high tea at some university, talking with other professors about modern art or ancient history. Only thing was, without killers like Spears and, yeah, like me, there weren't ever gonna be such places again. Maybe not anyhow.

Ahead of them, a pair of aliens stepped out of the shadows and hissed.

Wilks felt himself grinning. Fuck you, he thought. Don't you know me? You're messing with Doc Holliday, you stupid bastards.

He slid over next to Billie, who saw the aliens. They stood shoulder to shoulder and raised their carbines.

It got noisy in the corridor.

"Let's go, Powell. Stay with us."

The trio moved toward the hangar entrance.

# 20

The hangar was still patent, at least no aliens had managed to get in. After the two in the hallway, Powell's command override had admitted the trio through the lock without any other problems.

The vast space of the hangar was quiet, it seemed empty. If there had been work crews inside when the alert sounded, they were not around now.

"Which ship is the easiest to access?" Wilks asked. "Which one most likely to be fueled and spaceworthy?"

"Over there," Powell said. He pointed.

There might be other vessels elsewhere, but this particular hangar held four star hoppers, including the robot ship in which Wilks, Billie, and Bueller had arrived. Wilks was glad that the one Powell had indicated was not *The American*; he would prefer something with a little more human comfort designed into it. Then again, any port in a storm was a pretty good philosophy, and between Spears and the aliens, this place wasn't just a storm, it was a hurricane.

"All aboard," Wilks said. He waved his carbine at the ship.

The base was a wreck. Spears and his unit moved through the chaos, shooting whatever got in their way. Mostly, the targets were people; they did chop down a couple of the drones who were too slow on the uptake. What the hell, he thought, he was improving the gene pool. Attacking him was a nonsurvival characteristic, for certain.

There were few things to be salvaged here. He was going to have to cut his losses. True, he was going to win the battle and the war, pitiful and short as it was, but it would mean the base itself was a loss. Well. A good commander knew when to dig in or when to dump his tanks and leave the party. Third Base had served its purpose. He would have liked a little more time, but then, that was nearly always the case with commanders, wasn't it? You tried for perfect but you accepted what you had to and moved on. When the battle was joined, you had to deal with what *was*, not what you *wished* it was. In a perfect galaxy, you'd always have the troops and matériel you needed to wage the best battle plan. In this galaxy, it seldom happened.

The unit had lost a couple more troopers, one to gunfire, another to a booby trap, but it was moving well. The vault where Spears had his best drones stored, the cream of the crop so far, would be impervious to anything short of a nuke and only he had the key that would open the vault. Those being safe, the only other thing of value on this rock was the way off it. And he had that covered, too. It would be a poor general indeed who didn't keep his line of retreat open. Spears was not a poor general.

He led his troops toward the starship hangars.

Billie was beyond fear by now, her adrenaline surge no more than a trickle, just enough to keep her alert. It was odd to think that you could get used to something like this, but it seemed to be happening. Or maybe she was finally losing her mind. She was too tired to care which it was.

Next to her, Wilks said, "Well?"

He was talking to Powell, who frowned at the control unit he held. Powell tapped in a series of numbers on the small device, then looked at the ship the three of them stood in front of.

"The hatch isn't opening," Powell said.

"I can see that. Why not?"

Powell shook his head. "I don't know. This is the Command Override, it's supposed to open every lock in the base, right down to the beer coolers in the kitchen. It's the one Spears carries when he's here, it stays with whoever is the CO in the station. It has worked so far. It should work here."

"Are you sure you entered the correct code?" Billie said.

"Yes. I'm sure."

Wilks sighed. "Spears. He's fucked us again. We should have guessed it. As paranoid as he is, he wouldn't trust anybody with the ships if he wasn't around. We'll have to run a bypass."

"That'll take time," Powell said. "The access panel is armored."

"I don't see we have much of a choice," Wilks said.

Spears and his troops reached the outer hangar via the emergency escape tunnel he'd had built. The two transports in the huge room stood silent. He had half his platoon fan out and take up guard positions, but there was no need. They were alone. He almost felt sorry for the enemy. So outclassed. Powell never really had a chance.

"Okay, the rest of you with me to the inner hangar."

They moved down the interlink.

"I think that's got it," Wilks said.

The access panel for the hatch control had to be burned open, but once that was done, the circuits were fairly easy to reroute. Wilks bypassed the electronics entirely, shut off the power to the hatch, and used the manual crank to begin winding the hatch up. He had a fifteen-centimeter gap opened at the bottom when he heard the voice:

"Freeze frame it!"

Wilks turned to look, saw half a dozen marines in climate suits and full battle gear pointing their weapons at them. He spared a quick glance for Billie, and understanding passed between them. Better to go down shooting than to be fed to the aliens. "Good-bye, Billie," Wilks whispered. "Sorry."

He leapt for his carbine where it leaned against

the ship, saw Billie swing her weapon up to firing position. Wilks waited for the impacts of the bullets that would kill him, knowing there was no way he could get to his own piece before the marines cut him to pieces but going to go out trying. Fuck it—!

A blinding white light smashed into Wilks and took him away. Odd, he hadn't expected it to be like that . . .

When Wilks came to, he was lying on his back next to Powell, Billie sprawled on the other side of the major. Wilks blinked, not understanding.

"Nice try, Sergeant," Spears said.

Wilks rolled onto his side, found himself facing Spears. Half a dozen troops backed him, each of them holding stockstiks, essentially riot batons wired to stun a victim into unconsciousness at a touch.

"Concussion charges," Spears said, answering Wilks's unspoken question. "Mounted in the locks of all the ships. You'd gotten that hatch up another five or six centimeters, they'd have gone off without me having to use this." He waved a small electronic device.

Wilks looked at Spears, his mind still fuzzy. There was something he was going to do. What—?

"No point in doing anything heroic, Sergeant," the general continued. "I'll just have you stunned. You don't get to die, yet."

Spears looked at Powell, who had yet to awaken. "I might have known dickless there wouldn't have the balls to try something like this on his own. Was that you in the crawler shooting at my decoy?"

Wilks managed a nod.

Spears returned the gesture. "Thought so. You
get credit for trying, but you picked the wrong side.
Too bad. I admire a man with guts, even if he's an
enemy."

Billie moaned in her sleep.

"Win some, lose some," Spears said. He turned
away. "All right, men. You know the drill. Get the
cargo loaded, collect your gear. Sort out the prison-
ers and free the loyalists, I'll give you a list."

"What are you going to do?" Wilks said. His head
hurt and he felt as if he were going to vomit, but he
maintained, taking slow and deep breaths.

"Well, it doesn't really concern you anymore,
now does it? But because you gave me a decent
fight, I'll tell you. I'm going home, to Earth. I'll be
taking a small corps of the aliens and we'll have
ourselves a little sortie. Once I demonstrate how
effective my troops are, we'll get support to build a
full-scale army of trained aliens. We're going to
kick ass, son, and when I show the recordings of
how we did it to the powers-that-be, we'll get what
we need to *win* this war."

Jesus. He really *believed* it. The guy was a few
kilograms short of fission mass, crazy as a
stepped-on roach.

"What about us?" That from Powell, who had
managed to sit up.

"You and your allies are up for court-martial, Major. I don't have time to fool with such piddly shit
now, so you'll stay here until I can send the appropriate legal teams back to handle it."

"You can't leave us here! There are aliens loose
in the base! We'll be slaughtered, eaten!"

"You should have thought about that before you played at sedition, Major." He turned away and moved off.

Wilks made as if to stand, but two of the troopers stepped toward him, stun wands held ready. Wilks settled back. Jumping them would only get him another headache when he woke up in half an hour. If he woke up at all. Right now, it seemed a lot more important to stay awake. Whatever happened to them, he wanted to see it coming.

# 21

Mitch was on top of Billie, moving slowly and with great power, thrusting, filling her. Sweat beaded on his face and he held himself up with his arms, muscles corded in his triceps, connected to her only at the groin, the juncture of their sexes.

Naked, connected, they danced.

Billie had never felt so fulfilled, so complete, as a woman, as a human being. This was what she had always hoped for but never expected to have, someone who loved her, someone she could love in return, giving and receiving totally, becoming not less, but more than two—

Becoming one.

He moved faster, nearing his peak, and she moved with him. Yes. Yes. Yes, yes, yes!

He screamed.

Billie stared at his open mouth, saw the claw tear past his lips. But it did not reach for her, the taloned hand, it extended in a half circle on an arm too thick and long to have possibly come from Mitch's mouth, extended to his belly and tore into the skin and muscle, ripping him in two and hurling his top half away, leaving his hips and legs on her. White fluid spurted from the torn body, android blood the color of milk splashed over her in an obscene bath, hot, salty, even as he began to throb within her . . .

"No!"

Billie felt the pressure on her legs; she struggled to move from under the weight—

"Billie. It's me, Wilks. Wake up."

She blinked her way into consciousness. Her head ached, nausea filled her throat with a sour burning. Soldiers stood nearby, staring down at them from behind sealed faceplates, long rods held in their hands.

"Wilks?"

"Spears. We were hit with concussion grenades."

Billie didn't know what he was talking about. Where were they? The last thing she remembered, they were running. It seemed as if they had always been running.

"Billie."

"What?"

"Are you okay?"

Pieces of it came back to her. The aliens in the corridor. The ship door that wouldn't open. Men

with guns pointed at them, the unspoken decision
she and Wilks made together to fight.

"Yeah. I guess. What is going on?"

Powell, seated with his back to the wall, his
knees drawn up to his chest, said, "Spears is going
to load his tame monsters onto the largest transport ship and lift. He says he's going to Earth. We
get left here, along with all the other marines and
scientists."

"Hey, fuck that noise," one of the troopers standing next to them said. "*You* get left here with the
other traitors. Those of us who stuck by the general
are going with him."

Powell laughed, a sound on the edge of hysteria.
"Are you really that stupid, marine? He doesn't
need you anymore, you're excess baggage. You get
dumped."

"No way, Major," a second guard said. "Spears
takes care of his own."

"His own? Christ, he thinks he is fucking *God*,
you moron! You're nothing more than used toilet
tissue to Spears. You've served your purpose;
you're going to be flushed and compacted with the
rest of us."

The guards looked at each other. The leader, an
older sergeant Billie had talked to once, shook his
head. "Bottle it, boys. The major here is just trying
to divide and conquer. The general has taken care
of you so far, ain't he? Don't let this fubbie rattle
you. Didn't you hear the man tell you to pack your
gear soon as we get the traitors stocked away?"

The other five guards murmured. Billie thought
they still sounded unconvinced but it didn't seem

to matter. They weren't about to let the three of them go.

"Okay," the leader said. "Now that sleeping beauty is awake, let's move it, people."

Wilks got to his feet, helped Billie up. Two of the marines jerked Powell upright.

Billie saw Wilks gather himself. He was going to try to fight his way out. She didn't think he would make it, but she would follow his lead.

The lights went out.

"What the fuck—?" somebody yelled.

There was a zapping sound, like an electrical spark, and somebody moaned.

"Spookeyes," the sergeant in charge hollered. "Turn on your spookeyes!"

A long moment hung there, time suspended like a spider on a strand of glistening silk . . .

"Eyes on? Everybody see? Report!"

A chorus of assents.

"Nobody moves," the guard in charge said. "We're spookeyed and can see you like it was noon on the Equator."

The lights went back on, three times brighter than they had been before.

The soldiers screamed, almost with one voice. Their hands went up to slap against the closed faceplates. One trooper tore open the clear plate and dug at his eyes.

"What—?"

"Bueller!" Wilks yelled. He kicked one man in the belly, caught the baton he dropped before it hit the deck, whipped the stick against another man's throat. Even through the suit that must have hurt.

"Go, go! This way!"

Billie followed Wilks, Powell right behind her.

"What happened?!"

Wilks said, "They're blind. They got the hangar lights all of a sudden amplified a couple of million times by the spookeyes. Ordinary C-suits don't have blast shields in the faceplates; the military is too cheap to spend the money. It must have been like looking right at an atomic flash. Go!"

Once again, they ran.

Spears was personally overseeing the loading of the alien modules onto the transport truck from the vault when the frantic call came over the com.

"General, Powell and the other two have escaped!"

Spears felt a stab of irritation. He held it in check. "It doesn't matter. Penned up or running free, they are still going to be left here when we depart. Maintain watch, shoot them if you see them, but otherwise, let them hide."

After he discommed, Spears watched one of the modules picked up by the big hoop lifted and carefully stacked on the other modules on the truck. He was the only one who knew the access codes to the starships. Two of the vessels would be making the voyage in tandem, one with cargo, the second with but a single passenger—himself. The other starships would remain here. Terrible waste of matériel, but he couldn't worry about that. Sacrifices had to be made in war, be it flying stock or troops. A man who couldn't do the hot work didn't deserve to command. The engines of the ships that remained behind would be slag thirty seconds after

Spears departed. Whoever was left behind was going to stay behind, unless somebody came to take them off. And, given the unreasoning hunger the drone aliens had, it wasn't likely there'd be anybody left if anybody ever did show up here again.

He'd be taking the queen, of course, she was necessary to his plan. Control her and he controlled the drones. Some of the techbrains thought that a new queen could develop from a drone if there weren't any other queens around, but that wasn't likely here. The food supply on this mostly airless lump was pretty limited. The marines and scientists still alive wouldn't go a long way, unless the aliens had their own version of Jesus to do the loaves and fishes routine.

Spears smiled at that thought. The idea of the aliens with a messiah was funny. Then again, come to it, this group of creatures, of soldiers, might well consider *him* their messiah. It was true enough. He was going to lead them to a better world, to a kingdom of power and glory. Why wouldn't they think of him like that? Not that they did much thinking anyway, but then again, neither did human marines.

"Easy with that cargo," Spears said. "Don't want to hatch it before its time."

Not much longer. Too bad about the others at the air station, but that was how it went sometimes. The old adage about the best of battle plans not surviving the first engagement could apply here; still, it was a minor setback. Nothing a decent commander couldn't take in stride.

Spears grinned again. Soon as he lifted, he decided, he was going to smoke one of the special

cigars. Hell, he deserved it. He'd just won his first
battle in the war against the aliens. He'd still have
plenty to toke up once he won his first encounter
on Earth itself.

Yes, by God, he would.

"Now what?" Powell asked.

"Seems like I've been here before," Wilks said.

They were in an unused cargo area, empty car-
tons stacked in neat rows, forming a maze in which
they could stay lost for a little while, at least.

"We can run, but we can't hide," Wilks said.
"We've got to get off this planetoid or we're dead."

"How?"

"Spears will be taking the largest ship, my guess.
Maybe another one locked to it. We've got to find a
way to get onto one of the ships before he buttons
them up."

"How?" Powell said again.

"Do you know where the aliens he'll be taking
are stored?"

"A special vault, yes."

"Let's get to it."

"If anybody sees us—" Powell began.

"They'll shoot us?" Wilks finished. "Big fucking
deal, Major. Let's do it."

Spears rode with the first truckload of his precious cargo while his men continued to load the
next transporter. Nothing could go wrong at this
stage, he had to see to it personally. He had recap-
tured the queen easily enough, all he'd had to do
was find the place she was trying to hide her eggs
and wave a flamethrower at them. Once she was

caged, the wild aliens running around the base would calm down—at least until they realized she was gone. He had the walls of the queen's cage opaque so she wouldn't know where he was taking her until it was too late.

Everything was under control.

The vault was heavily guarded, the men loading the truck parked in front of the vault were heavily guarded, but the next empty truck fifty meters up the corridor had only the driver and two troopers sitting on it, doing nothing but waiting.

"That's it," Wilks said.

"That's what?" Powell said.

"Our ride. We can hide on that transporter, it'll take us straight to the ship Spears is using."

"You're crazy. We'll never make it."

"I'm open to a better idea."

Powell stared at him, then looked at Billie. She shook her head. "Wilks is pretty good at this stuff," she said. "He's saved us before. Whatever he says."

Wilks nodded at her.

"Okay. This is how I see it . . ."

Spears watched the containers being loaded onto the ship. All his plans were about to come to fruition. It was a glorious day for the Corps.

Billie, naked, stepped around the corner where the three men on the empty truck could see her.

"Jesus Christ," one of the men said. "Check this out."

Billie smiled, wet her fingertip with her tongue,

and touched her left nipple so it pebbled up and grew hard. Then she stepped back out of sight.

"Hey," one of the three troopers said, "wait up, honey!"

"You crazy?" the second marine said. "Spears will chew you a new asshole if he catches you gone!"

"It'll only take a minute," the first marine said.

"Spears—" the driver began.

"Fuck Spears," the first marine said.

"Nah," the second marine said, "I'm with you, I'd rather fuck her. Come on."

The two marines jogged toward where Billie had disappeared.

When they rounded the corner, they saw her standing there, legs spread wide, arms open, a big smile.

How could men be so stupid? she wondered. Did they really believe that a woman who'd never even *met* them would be so overcome with lust at the sight of them she'd strip to the skin and beckon to them, all wet and ready?

Apparently so. The two marines moved toward her, already dropping gear and untabbing their coveralls.

Wilks stepped out behind them and bopped each on the head with the wand he'd taken from the other guards. Both men fell, out before they hit the floor.

"Now we have guns and uniforms," Wilks said.

"Jesus, Wilks, are these the guys who have been protecting the civilized galaxy? No wonder the aliens are ahead."

Wilks grinned and shook his head. "What can I

say? If you can find the way to the test site, the galaxy's finest will let you join up. Get dressed."

"That was quick," the driver said when he saw the two marines approaching the truck five minutes later. "How was she?"

"I was great," Billie said, lifting her head and giving him a good view of her face.

The driver reached for his sidearm, but Wilks had his newly acquired carbine pointed at the man's heart. "You don't want to do that," he said. "Let's take a little walk."

Three minutes later, with Powell in the driver's clothing and the driver asleep and tied with the two marines in a closet down the corridor, the crew chief waved the empty truck into the loading area.

The chief knew Powell by sight, so the major kept his face more or less hidden. But the chief didn't know Wilks or Billie, they were just two more marines as far as he was concerned.

Spears watched the opaqued cage containing the queen being loaded. If the mother alien was upset, it didn't show, she was quiet inside the kleersteel box.

Once she was secured, Spears felt better. He spoke to a second lieutenant supervising the loading of the drones. "All right, once the last truck of cargo is loaded I want you to assemble the troops in B-hangar, gear packed and stacked and begin loading the *Grant.* I want every loyal marine onboard by 1600 hours, clear?"

The lieutenant's face brightened. "Yes, sir!"

"Carry on."

Spears walked toward his quarters. He had some items he wanted to pack himself. Once that was done, he would be ready. He smiled at the old adage he'd learned in his first tour. Once you leave a place, don't look back. There might be something there and it might be gaining on you. In this case there would certainly be something behind him, but it wasn't going to be following him, much less gaining. He was going to the glorious future; here was nothing but the dead past.

*Victis honor,* he thought. Let's hear it for the losers.

# 22

"What about Mitch?"

Wilks scanned the wide corridor as Powell drove the loaded truck, looking for somebody who might recognize them. So far, nothing.

"I don't know," Wilks said. "After that last stunt with the guards in the hangar, he'll have bailed out of the life-support control room—Spears would have sent troops to secure it. We're lucky he stuck around as long as he did."

"You promised we wouldn't leave him."

"Look, Billie, he's brighter than nine tenths of the troopers on this base and that probably includes me. He'll know we have to get off this planet. We don't know what Spears has in mind, exactly, but once he's lifted, whoever is left behind is history, probably pretty quick."

"We haven't seen any of the aliens lately," Billie said. "Maybe they're all dead."

"You don't believe that."

Powell cleared his throat. "Spears has probably gotten them back under control using the queen," he said.

"But Mitch—"

"Has got himself some dandy new metal legs and enough sense to know where they need to take him," Wilks finished. "He's probably hiding in one of the hangars already."

Billie fell silent. She wasn't sure how she felt but she didn't want to leave Mitch behind, that much she knew.

"We aren't going to just drive up to the ship, are we?" she said.

"I don't see why not. You keep your head down, nobody'll notice you. They're in a hurry, nobody is going to expect to see us driving the truck. We park, hop off, get lost in the shuffle."

"It seems unlikely."

"You don't know marines very well," Wilks said.

"He's right," Powell put in. "Everybody will be so nervous about screwing up and getting left behind they won't be working by the numbers."

Billie shook her head. She didn't think it would work but she didn't have any better ideas.

Pretty much everything material that Spears valued could be tucked into a single hardshell case. There was the pair of matched Smith & Wesson snub-nosed stainless-steel revolvers with custom wood grips, antiques that had belonged to a former South American tinpot dictator who'd set himself up as ruler on Lebanon II in the Khadaji System. Spears had pulled the weapons from the man's belt after he'd shot him in the head. Here were the carefully packed cigars, snug in their inert gas containers inside a padded plastic box. Next to the cigars, a reader and a small collection of read-only infoballs, military manuals and histories. A hologram of his basic training class on completion day. Probably most of them were dead by now. He had other things, of course, but nothing that couldn't be replaced. A soldier traveled best who traveled light, after all.

His packing done, Spears left his quarters and started for the ship. He did not look back.

Despite what he'd told Billie, Wilks was nervous. The hangar was huge and there was a lot of scurrying activity, but if something was gonna go wrong, it would be in the next few minutes. Well. A man did what he had to do and fuck the rest of it. At least he was armed now, and if he went down, he would go down fighting. There were worse ways to die if you were a marine. And being eaten from the inside out by an alien baby was as bad as anything he could imagine.

Two troopers using hoop-lifts were busy loading the aliens into the ship. The name stenciled on the side was CMC MACARTHUR.

"Pull around beyond the other truck," Wilks said. "Park it and step off on the opposite side, away from the loaders. There's a service bay forward, amidships, right?"

"Right."

"What do we do if somebody recognizes us?" Billie asked.

"Put them down. This ship is leaving. If we have to fight our way onto it, that's what we do. We can slag the hatch controls and lift right through the roof panel if we have to. Major? You got a problem with that?"

Powell shook his head but did not speak.

Wilks wasn't sure about Powell, but he didn't have a lot of choice about his allies at the moment. Billie, yeah. Bueller, if he showed up. Powell, well, he guessed he'd see.

The truck carrying its cargo of potential death rolled forward on its fat silicone tires.


Spears saw the last truck go past as he approached the ship. Another fifteen minutes and he'd be loaded and ready to leave. The first step toward his ultimate goal, the retaking of Earth.

The lieutenant he'd left in charge came up at a quick step. "Sir, the final transporter has just arrived."

"Load time?"

"Ten minutes, sir."

"Good, good. Once the ship is packed, you are to assemble the men at the *Grant*. The course has been logged in, you'll follow the *MacArthur* and the *Jackson* into orbit and we'll make the shift to E-space. Any questions?"

"No, sir."

"Good. Carry on."

Spears looked at the men loading the *MacArthur*. Nodded at one of them who glanced over at him. Strode away, toward the command ship *Jackson*.

•  •  •

Wilks and Billie were almost at the service hatch when somebody behind them called out.

"Hey, you three! What are you doing there? This area is off-limits!"

Wilks turned, ready to pull his carbine up and start shooting. But Powell moved into the line of fire between Wilks and the trooper behind them.

"At ease, trooper," Powell said.

"Major Powell?"

"That's right."

For a moment the young marine looked confused. It had been drilled into him from his first day in the Corps: If an officer says jump, you're in the air before you ask how high he wants it. But this was one of Spears's troops, and the major was no longer in command. The trooper's intellectual waters might be muddy but one thing was clear: A general outranked a major and the general was giving the orders.

"Keep moving, Billie," Wilks said softly. Since Powell blocked the marine guard's view, he slowly shifted his weapon, swung the barrel around carefully.

"You'd better come with me, sir," the trooper said.

"I don't have time for this, marine," Powell said. "General Spears and I have settled our differences and I've got business that cannot wait. Call him, if you like, but hurry it up."

From his angle, Wilks could see the trooper reaching for the bonefone control over his right ear. In another second he would be online with whoever was running the operations channel and the game would be over. Wilks now had his carbine aimed right at the trooper—only Powell stood right under the sights. Now or never.

"Powell, get down!" Wilks yelled.

The major was pretty quick. He dived to his right, hit flat on the deck, giving Wilks a clear line of fire.

The young marine was confused again. He didn't know whether to finish his opchan call or shoot. He tried to do both.

Wilks fired a single round, hit the man square in the middle of the chest. A clean heart shot. With the 10mm high-velocity slug, such a hit would usually put a man down pretty fast. The head and spine were better targets, but while a single shot might go unnoticed in all the mechanical noise and fuel venting in the hangar, a full burst would not.

The trooper went down, still looking confused. His carbine sagged. Went off. Half a dozen rounds blasted from the uncontrolled weapon, bullets *spanged* off the deck. Damn!

Powell, who was rolling, caught at least one of the slugs when he came up in the wrong place. Wilks saw the man's head explode.

When he'd been a boy, Wilks had once put a big firecracker into a watermelon. The effect of the bullet at this range was much the same as what had happened to the watermelon when the firecracker went off.

"Ah, shit!"

"Wilks?"

"Get in the ship, Billie. Fast!"

* * *

Seated in the control cabin of the *Jackson*, Spears got a call on the opchan.

"Sir, there has been some small-arms fire near the *MacArthur*."

Spears reached out and put the control computer online. "Cause?"

"Sir, we found Major Powell's body next to that of one of the sentries."

"I see. Any other activity?"

"No, sir. The *MacArthur* is loaded and sealed."

"Good. Let Powell's traitors bury him," Spears said. "I will be lifting off in three minutes. Clear the hangar and cut the gravity."

"Yes, sir."

Spears slaved the *MacArthur* to the *Jackson*, checked the codes to be sure the computer didn't have them wrong. Everything was green, all systems functioning properly. Overhead, the hatch covering the hangar began to slide back. He could feel the drone of the big pumps as they sucked the air inside the hangar into storage tanks. The gravity began to fade. A small tap on the repellors and the ship would rise. Once he was clear of the hangar, he would light the engines and boost into a slingshot orbit.

"Launch minus one minute," came the dry voice of the control comp.

The infocrawl on the screen sped by. The *Jackson* was clear to lift, the hatch over the *MacArthur* would be fully retracted in thirty-six seconds ...

Spears nodded to himself. Perfect.

* * *

Inside the ship, Billie and Wilks looked at rows of aliens in their containers, stacked on their sides in bins, three high.

"Christ," Billie said.

"Yeah. Come on, let's find the control room."

They'd taken half a dozen steps when the gravity faded considerably.

"Wilks? What is it?"

"I don't know. Maybe a malfunction in the station. Or maybe . . ." he trailed off.

"Maybe what?"

"Nothing."

"Come on, Wilks. Don't start holding out on me now."

"Could be we're about to lift. Inside a hangar they'll shut down the faux grav and use the repellors to boost, that's SOP so they don't fry the hangar with the engines' exhaust."

"We can't leave. Mitch—"

"I know, I know. Let's see if we can find the control room and do something."

With the gravity reduced to that of the planetoid, normal walking was impossible, they'd bound to the ceiling with every step. Wilks moved using a kind of swimming hop. He'd take a short, tiny step, grab something anchored, and pull himself along as if they were underwater. Billie figured it out pretty quick and it seemed to work.

They hurried toward the control room.


"Lift-off commencing," the computer said.

Spears felt a slight tug as the repellors kicked on, shoving the ship straight up. After a moment the repellors cut off and the massive ship drifted upward like a hot-air balloon on a cool and crisp morning. Spears touched a control. The external hardskin armor retracted and the inner polarized plate in the control cabin cleared. The blackness of space lay over the ship and planet like a shroud pierced with laser points.

He liked space travel, the sense of going vast distances to do great things. Made a man feel powerful, knowing he could conquer the galaxy that way, secure in his machine from the killer vacuum that would steal your air.

Can't touch me, he thought. He grinned at the vac for its impotency.

He switched another control on and got external cameras going. Put the rear viewer onscreen. Saw the *MacArthur* begin to rise from the base.

When the second ship was clear, Spears found another control, one that had not been installed when this ship had been built, a jury-rigged button atop a powerful transmitter. He had put that one in himself. He shoved the button down with his thumb.

Below, the engines of the remaining starships would begin converting themselves to molten waste. In less than a minute, what had been the acme of man's technology would be no more than a white-hot soup of swirling metal and plastic and electroviral matrices, all cooked beyond repair by anyone less than a god. And if God could fix them, he was one hell of an engineer.

Carefully, Spears opened the plastic box containing his cigars. He picked one from the middle of the box, pulled the tube out, twisted the airtight cap free. A tiny *whoosh* as the inert gas escaped, bringing with it the smell of a fresh cigar. He tilted the tube, removed the dark Jamaican Lonsdale, and looked at it with reverence. Worth a fortune, the dark-leafed beauty was about to go up in smoke. He smiled. Wasn't that the way of things? Even a great cigar would be nothing but ash after it was smoked. Things didn't endure. Only deeds lasted. And nobody had ever done a greater deed than to reclaim an entire planet from an enemy, and the motherworld of humans to boot.

He clipped the end of the Lonsdale with his cutter, wet the fragrant leaf with his lips, sucking on it lightly, then reached for his lighter.

The first puff filled his nostrils and sinuses and he blew it gently into the control cabin's cool air, watched the blue smoke pulled into the cleaners.

It didn't get much better than this, thought the savior of mankind. No, sir.

# 23

"**W**ilks!" Billie yelled. "Stop the ship!"

The gravity was gone, the ship was lifting, and Wilks knew there was no help for either from where he sat. The control board for the vessel was locked; nothing he tried got any response. Still, he tried.

"Wilks, goddammit, you promised—!"

"So fucking sue me! I can't do shit here! We're on automatic!"

Billie stared at him as if he had suddenly sprouted horns and a forked tail.

"This ship is probably slaved to Spears's," he said. "We go where he's going. I'm sorry."

She stared, not speaking.

Wilks sighed, leaned back, and pulled his safety straps tight. Okay, it was too bad about Bueller, but it wasn't his fault. He would have held the ship down for the android if he could have, but there was no help for it. It galled him to leave a marine from his unit behind, but he'd done it before. A lot of his comrades had died along the way. When your number was up, it was up. What the hell. Billie would probably come around to that view, and if she didn't, too fucking bad. Life was hard. She should know that by now.

Spears had his com on and it was only a matter of a couple of minutes before the frantic calls began to come through.

"General Spears! This is Pockler, on the *Grant*! There's been an engine malfunction! The ship is nonoperational, sir! We can't lift!"

Spears looked at the com. The transmission was no-pix, so he couldn't see the man's face, but he could tell well enough from the tone of voice how rattled the trooper must appear.

"General Spears? We're getting reports from the other ships, somebody has sabotaged their engines, too! Sir! Please answer!"

Spears took another puff of the cigar. God, this was a great smoke! He'd have to toke it all, of course, you couldn't smoke half and save it for later, it wouldn't store even in dead gas, not and be fresh like before.

"General Spears! Sir, we are trapped here! You'll have to bring the *MacArthur* back down!"

The ventilators sucked the used smoke away. He thought about shutting the things off and blowing a few smoke rings—they'd hang there for a long time in the greatly reduced gravity—but no.

"Sir, the alien drones have all gone crazy! They're hammering at the ship, they're everywhere, it's like they've lost their minds!"

Spears observed the glowing end of the cigar, held the thing up so the nearest intake vent could draw the ash away. Wouldn't do to foul the cabin with the residue, no matter how valuable it had been before. So, the aliens could tell that the queen was off-planet. Interesting. He wondered if the empathic connection was shut off by distance. Must be something like that. Mama had left and the children were upset. Most interesting.

"General—!"

But a good cigar, ah, now that was *really* interesting.

The ship's controls were locked but the com was operational. Wilks wasn't gonna be making any outgoing calls; he didn't want to take the chance somebody might overhear them—so far, he didn't think anybody knew they were here. And not that he had anybody to call, anyhow.

But somebody knew they were here. The board cheeped with an incoming, complete with visual.

Bueller.

Damn.

"Mitch!"

He didn't look any the worse for wear on the holoproj. Billie couldn't tell where he was, there was some bland officelike background behind where he sat behind a desk. His new legs weren't visible and if she hadn't known better, she would have thought he was as whole as when they'd met. So long ago. So far away.

"Hello, Billie. I've got this channel in a security pipe, computer-guided, nobody can overhear us if you want to talk. If you don't, I understand."

Billie looked at Wilks.

The marine shrugged. "Go ahead. Anybody figures out we're here, fuck it. I just realized this boat is like a pay ship, we're carrying the cargo Spears wants." He touched a control.

"Mitch, I'm here."

"I'm so glad to see you're okay," he said. "I was worried you'd been hit when the shooting started."

"You saw it?"

"I was across the way from you, yeah."

"Mitch, I'm sorry—"

"Not your fault," he cut in. "Spears has your ship slaved to his; you couldn't have stopped it without wrecking it."

"Can you get on another ship?"

He grinned, a small and tight expression. "Probably, though it wouldn't do much good. The troops all piled into one and the motor wouldn't start. My guess is that Spears slagged the engines. He doesn't want anybody following him."

There was a muted explosion in the background.

"What was that?"

"Grenade, probably. The alien drones left here are running amuck. Spears took the queen. I think they can sense that, somehow."

"Oh, God—"

"There's nothing to be done about it, Billie. I'm here and you're there. If there is a God, he or she or it has a warped sense of humor, from what I have seen."

"Mitch, I—I—"

"Don't, Billie. I have had some time to think about things and you're right. We're too different for it to have worked long-term. We'd have tried and probably beaten whatever we felt for each other to death sooner or later. It isn't just that I was made one way and you another. Our frames of reference are different. Even if we could have worked out all the stuff that went before, the ride wouldn't have lasted much longer."

"We could have made it last, if I hadn't been so afraid," she said.

He shook his head. Another explosion drifted up along the radio and television channels to where she sat watching him.

"No. The newer model androids, the really slick APs, maybe they've made the crossover into full-fledged humanity. Until I was torn apart by the alien, I could fool somebody's eye, that's all. I could even fool myself for a little while. In the end, I'm not really human, not in the same way you are."

Billie couldn't speak.

Wilks butted in. "You're better than we are, Bueller. That's your problem. Tougher, smarter, faster, and when it gets right down to it, more humane and more forgiving. If I were in your boots—if you still had any—I'd be royally pissed at what had been done to me. You're letting us off the hook too easy, man. Mitch."

Billie blinked and stared at Wilks. It was the first time she'd ever heard Wilks use his first name.

Mitch got it, too. "Thanks, Wilks," he said. His

voice quavered, he was barely able to choke the words out. Oh, God!

"You take good care of Billie."

"I will."

"Mitch."

"I've got to go, Billie," he said. "There are people out there dying and even though I've learned that not all people are worth saving, I still can't break that little built-in ethical rule. Take care of yourself, Billie. I love you. I realize now I always did. And for whatever time I have left, I always will. Good-bye."

The picture vanished before she could say it.

"Mitch!"

"Carrier's down," Wilks said. He stared at the blank spot where the projection had been. He wouldn't look at her.

If she'd been him, she wouldn't have looked at her, either. She felt like shit. Mitch was an android, but Wilks was right. He was a better person than she was. Much better.

She cried for what seemed like a long time.

"We've broken orbit and are moving at a pretty good clip," Wilks said.

Billie nodded dully but didn't speak.

"Probably we'll shift into Einstein space pretty soon. There are half a dozen sleep chambers in the forward crew section. The others have been torn out to make room for the aliens but those still seem to be in working condition."

Billie didn't speak to that, either.

"We should go down and check them out. No telling how long we'll be in transit once we shift. Could be months, years, maybe."

She looked at him. Her silence was getting on his nerves.

"Look, I already checked for a lifeboat. They took it out for cargo space. If they'd left it, we could have gone back. There are a few deep-space and C-suits, but they wouldn't do us any good. Even if we survived the trip down—and that's real iffy—we couldn't lift again. The aliens will eventually take over the base, you know that. Going back without a way to lift would be suicide. We couldn't help anybody."

"I understand," she said. Her voice was dead calm, flat, unemotional.

Jesus.

"Maybe when we get wherever we're going, we can make Spears pay for this," he tried.

She looked at him. "Whatever it costs him won't be enough," she said. Same tone.

"Maybe not. But it'll make me feel better."

After that, neither of them had anything to say for a long time.

In his bunk, tucked in with nothing more than accel-gee and a few bungies, General Thomas A.W. Spears slept, the peaceful sleep of a man without worry, a man without shame, a man without guilt. His rest was only a little disturbed by a pleasant, slightly sexual dream of war. He was riding with Stonewall Jackson, it was early in the Battle of Chancellorsville, before Jackson received the wounds that would take his arm, then later his life. "The Lord has given us this day in victory," Jackson said. Spears, who had nothing but contempt for any kind of religion, smiled and nodded. The Lord helped those who had the troops and the best strategy and tactics. But then again, victory was the key word, wasn't it?

Always. Always.

# 24

Wilks sat in what passed for a rec room on this tub, staring at the view of the *MacArthur* provided by the nose cam he'd managed to program to track Spears's vessel. The other ship was maybe half a klick ahead and slightly offset, relative to their ship. They could have been directly astern of the *Mac*, given that gee drives didn't spew dangerous flux, but the maneuver was an old one, adopted when such things had still been a problem.

Against the backdrop of blackness and pinpoints of unblinking stars, the other ship appeared frozen. There was no sense of movement, Spears's ship just seemed to hang there. Even the drone of their own engines was merely background sound, like being inside some big factory that throbbed but certainly wasn't going anywhere.

As in all military ships designed to be sailed or flown by men, the *Jackson* had certain supplies carefully stored away. Ship's rations weren't ever going to top anybody's culinary lists but you could survive eating them. There was enough food stashed to keep Wilks and Billie alive and even healthy for years, all the proper vitamins and minerals carefully included. That was assuming they stayed in normal space, droning along under the gravity drives.

Billie didn't talk much these days, but Wilks understood that. She was grieving, and the way he saw it, rightly so. He'd tried to warn her, back when he'd first seen it coming, but she hadn't listened. It didn't make him feel smug to think that he'd told her so. That was the problem with being older and maybe a little wiser in the ways of the galaxy. You thought you had something to offer, only thing was, almost nobody ever wanted to hear it. Billie was a kid, he was old enough to be her father. Not that he'd ever thought of himself as the fatherly type, but he had seen the grief between her and Bueller coming a long way off. He'd tried to tell her, to spare her, but she was like the new Colonial Marine recruits he'd seen over the years. Fresh, convinced that nobody had ever done anything except them, reinventing the wheel for themselves. They seldom said it but Wilks had learned to hear it in their unspoken thoughts: Old fart like you? What can you know, gramps? You were never young, or if you were, it was so long ago you've forgotten what it was like. Save your breath, old man, you'll need it to totter off to your grave. Fucking kids.

They were right about one thing, it was hard to remember when he'd been that stupid. He could

recall it, but it made him want to shake his head.
If he got stuck in a lift with the topectomy he'd
been at nineteen, he probably would throttle the
self-righteous little bastard after five minutes.
Three minutes.

"Wilks?"

"Huh?"

"What are we going to do?"

He shrugged. He could have taken her question
to mean a whole bunch of things but he knew what
she meant: What are we going to do about *Spears*?
The man was long past sanity, he'd left his troops
to die, had killed many of them himself, and was
now on a fool's errand that would certainly be the
end of them all.

"Wilks?"

"Right now, nothing. We don't have any arma-
ment, nothing to shoot with except the hand weapons, which don't do us any good against a ship like
that, even if we could figure out a way to hit it from
here. Oh, yeah, we could go EVA, we got a few
suits, but we're accelerating and there's no way we
can make up the relative speed. The squirt guns in
the suits won't push us hard enough.

"That's not to mention what would happen if
Spears decided it was time to make the leap into
Einstein while we were outside dicking around."

Billie blinked. He couldn't tell if she was really
interested in this or not, but he pretended she was.
"See, the drive fields pretty much follow the con-
tours of the ship generating 'em. If we were hugging the hull, maybe we'd go along for the ride. But
anything that stuck out, an arm or leg or a head,
maybe, would be left behind."

Billie blinked again, didn't speak.

"The field is better than any armor we've ever devised, you know, nothing gets through it, so we couldn't get back inside. So, even if we didn't get razored in half, there we'd be, outside the ship for however long we were in the warp. Months, a year, maybe longer."

"Maybe that wouldn't be so bad," Billie said.

"Maybe, if you don't mind running out of oxy and choking to death on your own $CO_2$. Then when the ship did drop back into n-space and eventually started to decelerate, our bodies would zip on ahead and probably spend eternity tumbling through space. There are better ways to shuffle off."

"And worse," Billie said.

"Yeah. There are worse."

"So where does that leave us?"

"Waiting. We can wreck this ship. Spears doesn't want that, not with his little army of monsters onboard. Maybe we can threaten him. Tear out the computers, get control somehow, ram the son of a bitch. Or maybe once we come out of the warp and start to slow down, we get a chance at something."

"Such as . . . ?"

"Hell, I don't know, Billie. I don't have all the answers. You got here at the same time I did. Maybe if you weren't feeling so fucking sorry for yourself you might come up with something!"

She stared at him. "You knew Mitch was an android. Before I ever met him, you knew. You didn't tell me."

Wilks glared back at her. "Yeah, and I tried to tell you to stay away from him, didn't I? You weren't having any of it. You can't blame this on me, kid. I did everything but lock you in your quarters to keep you away from Bueller. It never occurred to you I might know what the hell I was talking about, did it? Old chem-head twenty-year grunt, what the fuck could I know about anything, right?"

Billie looked down, said, "You're right. It wasn't your fault. I'm sorry."

He felt his anger evaporate. Jesus. Big tough marine, beating up on the little girl. "It's okay. I'm sorry, too."

That was all either of them had to say for the moment.

Before they could pick up the thread of the conversation again, the ship's warning buzzers sounded.

"Shit. That's the ten-minute signal. We're going into warp," he said. "Better get to the sleep chambers."

"What's the hurry?"

"Warp space does ugly things to your mind if you stay awake. I did half an hour once, part of a test group. It makes your worst nightmare seem tame."

She shuddered and he knew how she felt. They had both dreamed about the aliens too many times and those visions were horrible enough.

They hurried toward the sleep chambers.


Spears had three chambers from which to choose, all of which were functioning perfectly. He was normally not a triple-redundancy man when it came to his personal safety, but this mission was much bigger than a single human. Nothing must be left to chance at this stage.

He climbed into the center chamber. All three of

the hypersleep tubes had been rigged with special alarm systems. If any of the bioelectronics in his life-support system should malfunction, he would be awakened and given the command to transfer to another chamber by a recording of himself. Even if he were half-asleep he would understand the order well enough to make the change.

Not that he thought any such malfunction would happen, but if it did, he was prepared. In due course he would arrive in the vicinity of Earth. In due course he would choose the spot where the re-taking of Terra would begin. He intended that it be some historical battlefield: Gettysburg, the Alamo, Waterloo, perhaps the Plain of Jars or the ruins of El Salvador. Somewhere symbolic, to rally men behind him and his new army. He had considered a new place, somewhere untouched before by the mighty engines of war, but no. Standing on the shoulders of some historical giant would only add to his own stature. Besides, there were so few spots on Earth that had never seen any war. Offhand, he couldn't even think of one. Might as well choose a site with well-known glory.

As the lid of the chamber clamshelled down and the medical machineries hummed to life and connected themselves to him, Spears considered his choices. Iwo Jima. Hiroshima. Normandy. Cape-town. Bunker Hill. The Rio de Morte. Pearl Harbor. The Golan Heights. Baghdad. The 38th Parallel. Sparta. Rome . . .

So many places from which to select. What a wonderful thing war was . . .

# 25

Sleep:

The software of three human minds chemically shunted and spun Zen-like through the wet hardware of their brains with liquid neuronic flows, dendritic capacitors zapping, the subconsciousnesses singing hormonally to themselves.

Alone in a million-kilometer emptiness save for each other and things not human, they dreamed.

One mind was filled with joy. Two minds were caught in the clawed grips of horror. Of this latter pair, one faced certain death but fought valiantly, knowing Death would win. The other discovered she would live forever—but with the monster she faced as an eternal companion.

There was really no question as to which was the more terrifying dream. No question at all.

# 26

Billie awoke and for a moment didn't know where she was or how she had come to be there. Her back ached, her arms and legs were sore, her mouth was gummy. Puzzling, but in its own way, it was one of the happiest moments of her life: she had no baggage.

Then she remembered.

The lid of the chamber fanned up, the circulators kicked on, and a breeze of stale ship air wafted over her. She heard the *click* of Wilks's sleep chamber as the lid yawned like a hydraulic clamshell, saw him wince and turn his head as he came awake.

Wilks sat up, rubbed at his eyes, stuck his tongue out. He looked over at Billie and nodded. "Time to rise and shine," he said. His voice was a hoarse croak. "Another glorious day in the Corps."

Billie stared at him.

"That's what my old platoon sarge used to say every time we finished a session in one of these suckers," Wilks said.

"What happened to him?"

"Something he disagreed with ate him."

The two of them padded to the showers and cranked the sprayers on. Billie stripped unselfconsciously and stepped under the water. The spray was more of a drizzle but the water was hot and she felt some of the soreness from the months of sleep ebb under the warmth.

Wilks looked at her, taking in her nakedness, then turned back to let the water soak his hair and run down his face and body. Billie saw the scars on his body, some worse than the one on his face, marks of combat she supposed, either in wars or pubs or on some street somewhere. She wondered why he hadn't had the scars resected and wiped. Even with the marks on his body, he was in pretty good shape for somebody old enough to be her father. Nice ass.

Funny, she'd never really thought of Wilks that way, except in her nightmares. But that was more or less a standard feature of her dreams, had been since she was a kid. A monster tearing itself out of somebody she knew. All the more horrible because it had actually happened to some of the people she had known. Her parents. Her brother.

Wilks turned around to let the water play on his neck and back and Billie glanced down. If he thought of her in a sexual manner, it sure didn't show. It was kind of difficult for a man to hide that kind of reaction. Not that she had all that much experience with men, there had been a few, but one didn't grow up in a hospital without learning a little anatomy. She knew what went where, and what it had to look like before it could get there. There was no salute from Wilks to show any interest in her as a woman.

"How long were we asleep?"

Wilks, eyes closed against the stream of hot water, shrugged. "I dunno. I didn't check the meter. But if the ship woke us up, we must be close to where we're going."

"What now?"

"We finish our showers, get something to eat. Figure out our next move after that. One thing at a time."

Billie nodded, leaned forward a little so the water could trickle down her spine. Maybe that was the only way to get through life without going crazy. Take it one thing at a time, little bites you could chew without choking.

Spears made the discovery almost by accident. He'd been awake for six hours, had cleaned up and eaten a meal, dressed in ship fatigues and run a few system checks. This latter was more for his peace of mind than anything else, the ship's operational computer being sufficient to handle virtually all the chores without regulation from him. But being a careful man, he occasionally checked to be certain things were running as they should.

In this case, things were not running as they should. A tracking system on the cargo ship floating there a couple of klicks behind the *Jackson* said that two of the sleep chambers had been activated and utilized during the trip through hyperspace. Water had been drained from the storage tanks and then fed back into the recycler. Power consumption was up slightly from that necessary to maintain the troops in their suspension tanks. Oxygen consumption was also higher than it should be.

On the face of it, there were two scenarios that came to mind: one, a malfunction either in his computer or the internal systems on the *MacArthur*; or, two—

Somebody unauthorized was on that ship. They'd slept in the chambers, and were now breathing the air, drinking the water, and using the lights. There would be food stores being eaten, too.

Other than the drive, Spears had not thought to slave the ship's internal controls to his board, it hadn't seemed necessary. He had no eyes on the cargo ship, no way to shut down the air or power. True, he did have some weaponry on the *Jackson* capable of disabling or even destroying his companion vessel, but the last thing he wanted was for anything to happen to his precious cargo.

He leaned back in the form-chair and looked at the computer-generated infocrawl. All right. So there were a couple of stowaways on the ship behind him. No big deal. They didn't know he knew they were there. When he put down on Earth, he would take care of the problem before they knew what hit them. A pair of deserters, of frightened *human* troopers, wouldn't give him any trouble. A concussion grenade through the hatch and anybody standing around would be out of it. The tactical advantage was his. They were still a couple of weeks away from landing; he had plenty of time to plan the best way to take care of sniveling ship rats.

Meanwhile, there were other things to do. He had to get himself prepared for the coming battle. War was imminent. And about damned time, too.

Wilks exercised, using parts of the ship not designed for such activity but things that could be made to work. A thick pipe for chins. A pair of stools for dips and push-ups. Anything he could hook his feet under for crunches. He worked hard at it, harder than he would have had he been alone on the ship. That episode with Billie in the shower had called up a bunch of mixed emotions. On the one hand, he remembered her as a ten-year-old child, crying in fear as he saved her from the death her parents had suffered. On the other hand, standing naked next to her in the shower, he saw that she was a grown woman, attractive, and it had been too long since he had been with somebody that way. Billie had done it with Bueller, Wilks knew that.

But—Jesus. He was old enough to be her father. And for a brief time had more or less functioned in that role. True, he hadn't seen her for a decade or so after he rescued her, and that child and this woman hardly seemed related. Still, it wouldn't be good to let these thoughts continue. Not at all.

He finished his third set of fifty crunches. His belly burned, the muscles dancing on the edge of cramps. He lay on the deck, sweat beaded all over him. He'd been working out for about an hour, he was done. He'd run the water cold in the shower this time.

• • • •

Billie opened a meal packet. The reconstituted and heated food in the plastic container smelled like meat and gravy, with vegetables on the side, though it was all soypro.

Wilks entered the galley and nodded at her. She opened a second packet for him.

They ate in silence for a minute. It had been three days since they'd dropped out of warp. Wilks had spent much of the time exercising.

"Are you avoiding me?" she said.

He looked up from his food. "No. Why do you ask?"

"You seem distracted."

He stared at the brown goop in his container.

"No, I was just working on a plan, that's all. Thinking."

"Yeah?"

"Yeah."

"You want to let me in on it?"

"Well. It's a little rough."

"I'm not going anywhere."

"Okay. I'm pretty sure we're in the Solar System. I can't do shit with the instruments, they're all locked out, but it makes sense. With the gee drive it won't take long for us to get to Earth. Couple weeks, tops. We'll be moving along at a good piece of light-speed, and the last few days we'll be coasting, then using retro drive to slow down."

"All right, I follow that."

"So once Spears puts it into reverse, we're decelerating at the same rate. The ships, him, us. If we suit up and go EVA, we can use the suits' squirters to accelerate. We're all moving faster than a speed-ing bullet, but it's relative."

"So we suit up, jump off, and catch up to Spears. Then what?"

"Well, since he doesn't know we're here, maybe we surprise him long enough to make it there."

"Maybe?"

"Uh, yeah, he'll have proximity mass detectors. Plus radar and Doppler and luxflect. If he happens to be sitting in front of a sensor screen, he'll see us coming. Or probably there's an alarm rigged to tell him something is coming if he happens to be on the crapper."

"Then he shoots us to pieces, right?"

"Maybe not. Maybe he just cuts the retros and leaves us hanging in vac with no place to go. As-suming our ship doesn't splatter us like bugs on a flitter's windscreen when it 'speeds up' and zips on by."

"Why does this not sound like a good idea to me?"

"Or we could wait until we get where we're going and clonk him over the head when he opens the door to our ship to let his tame monsters out to pee."

"That's Earth, right, where there are a few mil-lion more monsters, none of them tame? No, thanks."

"All right. His detectors are likely set to pick up ship-size masses or stuff approaching at high speed, asteroids, space crap, like that."

"So?"

"If we catch up real slowly, maybe the system doesn't kick in until we're right on top of him."

"Sounds kind of iffy."

"I could go down into the engine room and take a hammer to the drive. If it didn't go spastic and warp us into a supercompacted ball, which it could, maybe we could disable it and make him come to see what's wrong. He doesn't want to lose this cargo."

"I don't like that plan much at all."

"Me, neither. So unless you got something better, I say we wait until he hits the brakes and then we go to him."

Billie sighed. "It's always something, isn't it, Wilks? Never boring, being around you."

"That's me. Life of the party."

In his cabin, Spears laid out his uniform for the initial upcoming battle on Earth. He'd saved one dress uniform, the billed cap with the gold braid and his star, the regulation black silks with his ribbons and medals, the evershine orthoplast over-the-calf boots. He'd wear a belt with his two antique revolvers, and the uniform's dress sword. Strictly speaking, of course, it wasn't SOP to wear dress blacks and ceremonial weaponry into a combatsit, but while he was going to be on-scene, he wasn't going to lead the new troops into battle. No, he would command from the rear this first time, he was too valuable to risk himself in this foray. Too bad. He'd never considered himself a REMF—a rear echelon motherfucker—no armchair commander. But in this case, he would have to forgo the pleasure of standing shoulder-to-shoulder with his men when the guns began to speak. He would be the most valuable man on the field not simply because he was the *only* man on the field, but because if something happened to him the war was over. Only he and the queen could command these soldiers and he could hardly trust her to continue the fight if he were gone.

No, he would stand back, this once, until he had more troops, more humans to help him. He was, after all, the commanding general of the Colonial Marines now, indeed, commander-in-chief of all military forces. And why not? Once he brought back records of his success, once he showed whoever was left how the job had to be done, who would dare to deny him the rank? And if anybody could be that stupid, a wave of his hand would remove the obstacle. Sic 'em, boys.

Spears smiled. It was all going so well. Aside from a couple of minor glitches back at Third Base, nothing the historians would linger over unduly, everything had run as smoothly as lube on glass. It was only a matter of days now. All the years of preparation were about to pay off.

He rehung the uniform, put the sword and boots away.

He had decided to land in South Africa, a northeastern section of which was once called the Natal province. In the late 1800s, the area had been ruled by a native named Cetshwayo, who commanded a large army of warriors known as the Zulu. They were fierce fighters, the Zulu, and there had been a lot of them, but even so, they'd been no match for the technologically advanced British when it came to war. In one famous battle, a small unit of British soldiers withstood an assault against a vastly superior number of Zulu for some days, due to their better weapons, tactics, and training.

Spears related to that. A tiny force, well directed and focused stopped an entire army. All things being equal, it was the commanders who decided battles. The aliens were fierce, savage, hard as iron, but they fought like ants. They had not learned the arts of war as had men, and few if any men knew those arts as well as Spears did.

Give me a lever and a place to stand and I will move the galaxy, Spears thought. He had his place. His lever flew in the ship behind him. He was so full of anticipation he could hardly breathe.

# 27

"**Y**ou awake?"

Billie rolled over on the pad and looked up. She was in her underwear, the room was warm enough so she didn't need any covers. Wilks stood there, dressed in a spacesuit liner, white stretch that fit him like paint.

"I am now."

"We're decelerating," he said.

"Oh, shit."

"Yeah. Time to get dressed for the party, kid."

Only a week away now, Earth loomed large ahead of Spears. He tried to settle down with a history of the Gladitorial War, but the text did not hold his interest. Over the years he'd forced himself to learn patience, to wait, but it was hard now that he saw the goal so tantalizingly close. Here was the light at the end of the tunnel, the finish line for a race run long and hard. He found himself staring at the image on the viewer and when that wasn't enough, lifting the outer armor and looking directly at the distant planet through the thick, hardened glass.

Don't worry, I'm coming to save you. I'll be there soon. A few more days and your liberation will begin.

Wilks knew he couldn't think of everything that might go wrong. And even if he *could* he didn't really want to anyhow. If he knew all the pitfalls, he probably wouldn't go. But hey, fuck it. If you sat around worrying all the time, you'd never get anything done. Get a plan and move on it, that was the way.

The two of them stood in the lock, mostly suited, carrying what they thought they would need. Strapped to them with cro-tape were extra oxy bottles, their carbines and ammo, all the squirters they could find. They were joined to each other by a three-meter length of cable, connected to lock rings on the hips, his on the right, hers on the left. There wasn't really any way to judge their relative speed once they left the ship, hell, even while they were on the ship, but Wilks was hoping to move slowly, to make up the two klicks or so in an hour, no faster. They had enough air for three hours and if they hadn't managed to get inside Spears's ship by then, well, too bad. Wilks had rigged both suits with grenades from the carbine's launcher. If he ran out of air, he wasn't going to choke to death slowly out there. Move a protective cover and a

sharp rap with the suit's pliers and boom, end of
story.

"Billie?"

She was fiddling with her crotch plate, still un-
sealed.

"I can't get this damned plug in right. Do I have
to use it?"

"Unless you want yellow globules floating up in
front of your eyes if you have to pee, yeah."

"Doesn't seem fair to me," she said. "This operation must have been designed by a man."

"Nature of the plumbing, sorry. You need a
hand?"

There was a moment of silence.

"Maybe not," she said. "If you do that, maybe we
won't get out of here for a while."

Well, there it was. Wilks nodded, managed a
smile behind his faceplate. So the thought had
crossed her mind, too. Made him feel a little better,
for some reason he couldn't quite figure out. Kind
of like, well, if they both saw it, they didn't have to
follow up on it.

Billie returned his smile, and Wilks felt as if she
understood what he was thinking.

"I've got it," she said. "Yee, it's a cold little devil."

"It'll warm up. You ready?"

"As I'm going to get, yeah."

"Okay. Seal it up and start your air flow. Might as
well get this show on the road."


Billie smiled at Wilks's back as he moved to the
outer door to open the lock. So that's what all
those push-ups were all about. He'd thought about
sex, too.

Maybe in this case the thought was better than the act. Not *doing* it, but afterward. Somehow the idea of waking up next to Wilks the morning after seemed utterly strange. And maybe what she had felt had something to do with putting her life on the line again. That urge to reproduce yourself when you thought you weren't going to be around much longer. She'd learned about that in a class at the hospital. It was, so they had said, a common reaction to near-death experiences, especially in sudden and violent confrontations with the grim reaper. Something about releasing stress.

The hatch slid open. A little flurry of air blew out and turned into white crystalline swirls. Wilks stepped out, used his magnetic boots, and stood on the side of the ship, sticking out like a thorn on a stem. Billie followed him.

When they were both outside, free of the ship's faux grav, Wilks turned so that his back faced the distant dot of the other ship. "You okay? Don't speak, just nod or shake your head."

Billie nodded. He'd told her they'd be using line-of-sight laserlight coms, short range and focused in the same direction that the speaker was looking. That was so Spears couldn't overhear them. If you can see Spears's ship, Wilks had said, don't open your mouth, don't say a word. The coms were supposed to be good for a couple hundred meters, no more, but you never knew. If he knew they were out here, it could get real tricky real fast. If she wanted to speak to him, they had to take turns looking away from the *Jackson* when they did it.

Wilks clumped along the side of the ship. Without anything to relate to, up and down didn't have much meaning, and Billie quickly adjusted her mind-set so it seemed she wasn't walking on the side of the vessel but on top of it.

It took a couple of minutes to get to the front of the *MacArthur*. When they were perched on the nose like flies on the end of a banana, Wilks turned around to look at her. "Okay, you remember the drill?"

Billie nodded.

"All right. Cut the power to your boots and use the squirter, on three. One . . . two . . . three!"

Billie shut off her magnetics and triggered the squirter. It looked like nothing so much as an indoor plant sprayer; there was a narrow neck with a lever, a kind of handguard loop over that, and underneath, a small thick plastic tank with the compressed gas in it.

The squirter tried to pull itself out of her hand, but she tightened her grip and stiffened her arm and was lifted clear of the ship. She twisted slightly, saw Wilks pointing behind them, and aimed her squirter that way and depressed the control again.

The gas made faint sparkles as it spewed and froze.

It took a little adjustment but after a couple of minutes she and Wilks evened out and flew side by side, the thin coil of line connecting them left a bit slack. He faced forward more than Billie did, but she could shift her head enough inside the suit to peripherally see the ship ahead of them. All too quickly their own ship seemed to drop into the distance behind them, dwindling to the size of a toy model.

Wilks puffed out a couple of short bursts on the squirter and turned himself so he could speak.

"Might as well relax and enjoy the ride," he said.

Billie nodded. She realized she was breathing too quickly and made an effort to slow that down. It really was something, to be floating along in the middle of nowhere like this, soaring like some magical bird across the bleakness. Whatever else happened, this was truly something.

Unable to sleep and knowing he could not allow himself to become exhausted at this stage of the invasion, Spears used a soporific popper. The medicine felt cold as it blasted through the skin over the crook of his elbow. Within a minute he was feeling drowsy. He decided to fall asleep watching the approaching Earth, now a small half ball lighted on the "top." That meant the sun was "above" it, relatively speaking, and bright enough even at this distance to cause the polarizers to darken the glass.

The drug washed over him and he drifted on chemical tides into the doldrums of Morpheus.

Wilks could make out details on the ship; he guessed they were maybe six or seven hundred meters away. He'd already slowed them down twice, and it seemed they were still moving too fast, but now he figured they were either going to make it or they weren't and fuck it.

He'd laid it out for Billie that they were going to try for one of the aft locks. His reasoning was that if Spears was forward in the control area, where he ought to be, checking his damned sensors if he heard them coming, then it would take him a minute or two to get from the front of the vessel to the rear. It wasn't a huge ship, but there wasn't any reason for him to go aft unless he thought somebody was knocking on the door there and maybe that would buy them enough time. More iffy shit, but hey, there it was.

Once they got into the ship, if they did, they'd shuck the suits, grab their carbines, and take Spears out.

That was pretty much as far as Wilks had gotten with his plan. He assumed that Spears was alone, Bueller had seemed to confirm that, but maybe he had company. A bedmate or somebody. They'd look real carefully, if they got that far.

Still, Wilks was optimistic. They'd gotten *this* far, hadn't they? With some pretty good odds against them, they were still alive. Maybe they had a patron god with nothing better to do than watch out for them. Or maybe all the good luck was about to go sour. No way to know, nothing to do but keep on going.

Billie realized as they neared the ship through the void that she wasn't ever going to get used to this. She had avoided death for what seemed like dozens of times in her life, from Rim until now. Somehow, she expected that she would become acclimated to it, like getting into a soak tub that was a bit too hot. Once you settled in and got still, your body adjusted itself.

That wasn't happening here. The rush of adrenaline through her, her rapid heartbeat and too quick breathing, those were the same. Her bowels twisted, her mouth was dry. And it was a good thing Wilks made her put that urinary plug in. It was as if fear had her in its grip and was squeezing her tightly. The closer they got to the ship, the more Billie wanted to turn and run away. Her conscious mind knew they had to do this, but some deep part of her, way beyond the Billie who was usually in control, that part wanted her to find a deep hole and crawl into it. *Leave*, it said. *Flee! Hurry, before it's too late!*

On the one hand she was more fatalistic about survival; on the other hand she was just as scared of dying. Not the dying itself so much as the way of it. Going to sleep at a hundred ten or twenty, surrounded by your family who loved you, grandchildren, great-grandchildren, that was not so bad. Being eaten by a mindless alien monster or running out of air in space were not such pleasant ways to end one's short life.

But there was nothing to be done for it. It was take the risk now and maybe die or for certain die later.

*Wait until later!* her inner voice screamed. *It's always better to wait until later!*

Spears stood near the new road built by the Royal Engineers at Laswari, the dark earth packed and rutted by the passage of horse-drawn cannon. Sir Arthur turned to him and said, "Well, old man, what do you think? Can we stop the bloody buggers?"

Spears nodded. Sir Arthur wasn't yet the Duke of Wellington—how Spears knew he would be wasn't quite clear—but in the matter of the fight against the Sindhia and Bhonsle families of the Marantha, he knew the Indians would lose.

"We'll stop them."

"Then let's have at them, shall we?"

Sir Arthur waved at his officers, who had been watching him carefully for the signal.

The cannons opened up, the muskets began to speak.

God, Spears loved the smell of black powder in the morning.

The wails of the dying Indians began to float over the battle scene. The screams of one poor soul in particular rose louder, a rapid series of yells, as though the man were screeching, pausing for breath, then repeating the same monotonic noise with machinelike regularity. Aaahh! Aaahh! Aaahh . . .

Spears awoke to the sound of the proximity alarm's intermittent and nerve-jangling wail. In his drugged sleep fog, the sound made no sense to him. He reached out and slapped the shut-off control. Closed his eyes. He had incorporated the sound into his dream . . .

Spears struggled against the grip of the chemical urging him back to slumber. The proximity alarm.

There was nothing threatening through the glass in front of him. Despite all the high-tech gear, that was the first place Spears looked, through the window. Then he began operating the sensor board.

Nothing showed on the radar or the Doppler screens when he brought them up. But it didn't take long to get the log showing what the problem was. Two man-sized objects had come to rest aft on the *Jackson*. A quick extrapolation determined that they had come from the *MacArthur*.

As if there were anywhere else they could have come from.

Well, well. His ship rats had decided to pay him a call. Obviously they were braver than he had figured. Odd, he hadn't thought any of his troops would have been so—

Spears grinned. Of course. He knew who they were. That damned sergeant! And since Powell was dead, it had to be the woman with him. Amazing. If in fact this was them again, they had more lives than a cat.

Spears was glad they were here. This way he could eliminate them without any risk to his cargo.

Quickly he stood, grabbed the belt with his sidearm, and started aft. He didn't know how long he'd slept after the proximity alarm had started blaring, but it was long enough for them to arrive on the ship's hull. Since the locks weren't coded to keep people out—who would expect visitors in deep space?—then they'd get onboard. He had to kill them before they did any damage—

He slowed his pace. Hold on a moment. He had to figure they'd be armed, that they knew who was in command of this vessel. If he went barreling in, he might well be shot. That wouldn't do. He stopped. No, cowboy heroics were not the way to go here. They were pests, he would treat them as such.

Spears turned around and went back to the operations board. Unlike the *MacArthur*, he *did* have

control of everything on this vessel. Air, power,
even gravity. The rats had walked into a trap, only
they didn't know it yet. Time to roll the recorders
again. The military historians of the future would
love this.

# 28

"Now what?" Billie said. "Can we get out of these suits?" She had her faceplate open, as did Wilks, so they could talk, but it would only be the work of a second to slap it shut and seal it.

"No. Because Spears hasn't come blasting through the door doesn't mean he doesn't know we're here. You can shuck the extra gear but keep your weapon ready."

Wilks was already checking his own carbine. The dry lube used in the mechanical part of the weapon was supposed to be more or less impervious to high or low temperatures but he cycled the action and ejected a couple of live rounds to be sure. It wouldn't do to have the damned thing frozen solid by the cold vac if Spears did show up waving a gun of his own.

"Okay, mine works," Billie said.

"Good."

"What now?"

"Now we wait a little while and see what he does. If he knows we're here, he'll do something."

"Or maybe he'll rig another concussion grenade like he did back on the base and wait for us to walk through and trigger it," she said.

"That's possible. That's another reason for us to stay here and wait. Nothing happens for the next hour or so, we'll work our way forward. Carefully."

Billie nodded. "You're in charge."

Wilks nodded back at her. Yeah. He wished he felt as good about it as he tried to sound.

Spears finished his preparations. He had to assume that the sergeant—what was his name? Watts? Jenks? something—was a good enough soldier to do a basic recon before embarking on anything precipitous. If he were him, he'd assume he'd been spotted on arrival and suspect that his enemy was prepared for him. Which was true. In the sergeant's boots, Spears would dig in, find a defensible position, and wait for his opportunity to take the opposition out. A single well-placed shot would do it. The sergeant must be hoping Spears would make a foolish misstep and give him the chance.

Sorry, marine, not this time.

Too bad he was no longer interested in leading human troops. This sergeant would make a good officer, he was brave, smart, willing to take chances. In another lifetime, Spears would have bumped him up in rank and been glad to have him in his service. And he was certain, even though he had not seen him, that one of the two hiding down in the aft cargo area was ... Wilks, that was his name. Wilks.

Spears offered the unseen enemy a sketchy salute. Better luck next incarnation, son.

He moved to the attack.

Billie hunched down across from Wilks, trying to hide behind a modular cargo container, empty, it seemed, and to get comfortable in the spacesuit. She didn't think she managed to do either very well. The suit hadn't been designed for such contortions and the joints didn't bend easily.

They were in a place where they could watch the hatch leading into the bay from the rest of the ship. The only other ways in or out were through external hatches, and while he didn't think Spears would try that, Wilks had fixed those portals so they couldn't be opened from either side anymore. Nobody was going to sneak up behind them, he'd said. And nobody was going to be leaving that way, either. Not without a lot of work first.

Waiting for something to happen was driving Billie closer to the edge every minute. She hated this.

Suddenly it got dark. And when she jerked around to look for Wilks, Billie floated up into the air. Shit—!

"Billie, close your faceplate! Now!"

Wilks reached up and slapped his own plate shut, then reached for his oxy feed. He heard the door to the corridor slide open on its track, and he tried to bring his carbine to bear that way. It was hard to do in zero gee. Spears had cut the lights and gravity, probably the air, too, and Wilks guessed he would either shove a gun through the door—bet your ass *he* was braced when the faux grav shut down—and hose the room, or maybe toss a grenade inside. It wouldn't be anything big, nothing that might hole the ship.

Concussion bomb, maybe a little fragger.

The suits wouldn't even slow down the shards of a fragger, much less a 10mm caseless. Damn, damn, *damn!*

When the timer shut off the power and air and faux grav on the *Jackson*, Spears was in position. Even if they were braced for an assault the cessation of weight ought to throw them for a moment. Long enough to lob a concussion grenade into the hold. Once they were out, it would be the work of a moment to finish them.

The door slid open. Spears, braced and holding himself down, tossed the grenade through, then pulled himself out of the doorway and flat against the wall. Some of the blast would enfilade back through the opening, of course, but he wouldn't be in its path. Without gravity to slow it, the grenade would sail a long ways before it hit a wall and bounced back, it was possible it could come straight back out the door, he supposed, but that wasn't going to happen, because the grenade's fuse was a short timer and in about a second . . .

The gravity came back on. Spears was prepared for it. The thumps inside the hold told him his enemy had not been. He grinned—

•  •  •

The emergency lighting had been suppressed, of course, but the tiny red and green power diodes mounted next to the door's control panel were battery-powered. They didn't put out much light, but there was enough of a glow for Wilks to see something moving fast in the doorway.

He was still half a meter above the floor and twisting and to shoot the carbine would produce enough recoil to move him like a small rocket would; still, he had to do something.

Wilks shoved the carbine toward the door. He squeezed the grip and thus lit the laser sight. The tiny red dot danced crazily across the doorway. When it disappeared, he figured he was as lined up as he was going to get. He fired.

The recoil spun him through the air, like a wobbly planet on its axis—

Billie saw the muzzle flash from Wilks's gun, a spearhead shape of red and orange. The light from the blast showed her where he was, but he vanished in the dark immediately after the flash died. Her helmet muted the sound somewhat. She heard the bullet *spang* against something past the door. She thought. It was so dark—

A brilliant light splashed her, strobing the hold, then something heavy thumped against her, knocking her backward. She flew like a bird with an injured wing, tumbling.

The gravity came back and she fell to the deck, slid a little, stopped—

Jesus—!

•   •   •

Spears knew carbine fire when he heard it, and the bullet punched through the wall behind him and to his left as he shifted his regained weight to a careful stance. The shot and the grenade's blast came almost together. He'd wait a second and see what happened—

Wilks hit the deck hard, landed on one shoulder. He rolled to a prone firing position, thrust the carbine out, and found the laser's dot against the far wall next to the door. On the chance that Spears might be flattened against the wall there, Wilks opened up and drew a dotted line from the wall across the doorway to the opposite flanking wall. He fired on semi-auto, for control. He hoped Billie had enough sense to stay down, wherever she was—

A round burst through the wall between Spears's body and his arm. A few centimeters either way and it would have hit him. Damn! The grenade had missed them!

The bullets chewed fist-sized holes, moving away from Spears, spraying insulation and bits of wall plastic as they mushroomed and tumbled.

Time to regroup, he thought. His initial attack had been thwarted. He knew when to cut his losses.

Spears slapped the door control. The door slid shut. He moved away quickly, toward the blast door a few meters up the corridor. Once on the other side of that, he stopped. He lowered the door. This hatch had been designed as a pressure safety device. It was airtight, constructed of duralloy, and capable of stopping something as puny as assault rifle fire.

From his belt, Spears pulled a spot welder. He lit the arc and braze-feed, and ran a bead along the base of the door. To be sure, he added a half meter on each side. Then he opened the control box and slagged the electronics. Finally, he lifted the manual safety hatch and welded the crank handle to the steel safety cage. This door wasn't going to be opened from the other side unless somebody had a cutting torch and he didn't think Wilks was that prepared. But just in case, he set two fragmentation grenades on stik blobs to the wall at eye level and ran a trip wire. If by some miracle they managed to raise the door, a careless step would get them. And he rigged the trip so it was three meters away from the doorway itself. They'd maybe look for a wire on the way through, but probably not so far away.

Not, he thought, that they would ever get through in the first place.

He couldn't micromanage the gravity on a ship this size, but he could keep them cold and in the dark, without air. Even if they had their own air supply, they couldn't last more than a day or two.

Ah, well. Better shut down the recorders. This hadn't come off quite as neatly as he had hoped. No problem. A win was a win. It might not be pretty, but they were bottled up back there and that was the end of it. He gave them credit for trying, but close wasn't good enough for a cigar.

Spears laughed softly at his own joke and went forward.

•   •   •

Wilks and Billie had the suit lamps lit, so they could see each other okay. It was dark and it seemed to Wilks already getting cold and stuffy.

"Might as well breathe his air for as long as we can," he said. "When whatever is already in here is gone, that'll be it. We're back to the tanks. Shit."

"Wilks? Are we screwed?"

"Yeah. He's dropped the pressure door down the hall. Fucked the controls up. He must have known we were coming all along. We're lucky the concussion bomb didn't get us, but yeah, we're screwed. We ain't going anywhere now."

"Can't we get outside the ship?"

"Maybe. I could probably manage to unseal the hatch we came in if I tried hard enough, but the minute we step outside he'll shake us off like fleas from a steel dog. We'd never find another way in in time."

"Can we blow the ship up?"

He looked at her. He understood the thought. If they were gonna die anyhow, might as well take the bastard with them.

"I don't think so. This is a military-grade vessel. I could set off what grenades we have but it wouldn't do much more than ruin the aft section, if that. These ships are built in segments, airtight compartments. We could take out some inner walls, but segments are armored like the hull. The drives are amidships and out of reach. Even if we did cripple it we'd die as a result, and he could probably just transfer to the *MacArthur* at this point."

"So that's it?"

"Well, we might get to the oxy stores buried in

the walls here and bypass his control. We might get enough air to last a couple more days."

"But not to get to Earth."

"That would be my guess."

"Damn."

"Sorry, kid. We tried. We lost. That's the way it goes sometimes."

"Nothing we can do?"

"Not unless we can convince Spears to turn over the keys to the escape pod."

"Maybe if we said 'please'?"

Wilks thought about that for a second. "Hmm. I got a better idea. Maybe if we said 'or else.' "

"Hello, General Spears," said the voice from the com. It was on the suit radio opchan, right where he thought it would be. Spears leaned back in his form-chair and nodded at the com. "I was expecting you to call, son. Nice try but you lose."

"Maybe, maybe not. Billie and I, we were hoping you could see your way through to cutting us loose."

"What would be the point, marine? It's a long walk home. You'd never make it."

"We could if we had one of the two escape pods."

Spears grinned. "That you might. But I'd have to give you one and I don't really see that as a possibility. Nothing for me to gain."

"We'll trade you for it."

"Son, you don't *have* anything to trade."

"How about nine linked M-40 grenades, all set to go off at once?"

"So you blow out the ass of the vessel and kill

yourselves, it won't even dent the armor amidships. Nice try, but you ought to know better."

"Oh, I didn't mean I had the grenades *here*, General."

Spears leaned forward. "What are you talking about?"

"Well, Billie and I, we figured you were pretty good when we flew up here. Given our experiences so far, we had to bet there was a good chance you'd take us out."

"Good bet."

"Yeah, well, you're a general and I'm a sergeant. But we figured, what the hell, if we died, we could have the last laugh."

"Keep talking." He had a feeling he knew where this was going and it sent a chill through him.

"So before we left, I rigged a little explosive in the *MacArthur*. Kind of a going away gift, you know? With a timer. We gave ourselves plenty of time to get here and beat you, plenty of time. Got an hour or so left."

"You're bluffing."

"I can see how you might think so. But we aren't. And can you take the chance? If we *did* wire the ship, your tame monsters get an E-ticket ride to nowhere in about fifty-eight minutes. Your command, General, adios forever."

Spears stared at the com. Wilks was bluffing, he was pretty sure. But if he *wasn't* . . .

Damn. Could he take the chance?

"Now if you want to trade, here's the deal. You cut one of the pods loose, within the next two minutes. That way you don't have time to go and play with it. Billie and I, we leave the ship, rendezvous with the pod, and radio you the location of the bombs. You can get to the ship and deactivate them in the other pod easy enough, with twenty minutes to spare."

"Assuming I believe you and do this," Spears said. "What's to stop me from blasting you and the pod into atomic dust with my ship's guns the second you radio me the location?"

"Your word that you won't."

Spears grinned wider. "My word?"

"You're a man of honor, aren't you, General?"

"Of course, son."

Spears chewed at his thumbnail. He couldn't take the chance that Wilks was telling the truth. Not with his army at risk. Besides, once they were outside the ship and in the pod, he could pot them easy enough. As long as they were in the aft cargo bay, they might figure out some way to get out and into the rest of the ship. Damned fucker was resourceful.

"All right, marine. You have a deal."

Billie grinned at Wilks. "He bought it!"

"We ain't home free yet," he said, but he grinned back at her. "He'll probably plan on taking us out with the ship's guns as soon as we're in the pod."

"What about his 'honor'?"

"Are you kidding? He's a sociopath, he's got as much honor as a spider."

"So how do we stop him from shooting us?"

"I have an idea. If we're fast and lucky, it'll work. If not, we're no worse off than we were before."

"I'm with you all the way," she said. "It's not like I've got another engagement or anything."

• • •

Once they were inside the escape pod, a small ship capable of a couple of weeks of cramped flight, it wasn't twenty seconds until the com lit with the incoming call.

"All right. Where are the bombs?"

Wilks was busy putting the drive system online. He powered up the small engines, activated life support. "Strap in," he ordered Billie.

She obeyed. "Where are we going? There's nowhere to hide out here."

"Yes, there is. Watch."

He tapped a control and the little ship moved forward.

"Wilks, I want the location of the bombs now or I will cancel our agreement and blast you."

"Too late," Wilks said as the pod moved almost back to where it had been launched from the ship.

"What good does this—?"

"His guns are on top, the sides, and under the nose," Wilks said. "His field of fire covers a full sphere, but there aren't any guns directly under the pod launch bay and he can't elevate or depress any of them enough so he can accidentally shoot himself. Or, in this case, us."

The tiny ship rode a few meters away from the larger vessel.

"Can we stay here?"

"Not for long, he'll start playing with the drives and we'll lose contact. But he can't wait, the clock is running. Hold on."

Wilks touched the com. "General, you want to go to the power control box for the aliens' tanks, the main cable from the generator to the control cabin where it leaves the forward circuit breaker and the gee drive housing next to the gyroswitch complex."

"Damn, I thought you were bluffing."

"No, but I lied. You've got about ten minutes to pull the charges, not twenty. If you dick around trying to shake us so you can chew us up with the *Jackson*'s guns, you might not have time to save the *MacArthur*."

There was a moment of silence.

Then, "You would have made a good line officer, son. You got more guts than a slaughterhouse."

"Thank you, General."

"All right. You can tell your grandchildren you went up against me and survived. That'll mean something someday."

To Billie, Wilks said, "Hang on."

With that, he turned the pod so it faced the ship two klicks behind them and hit the thrusters full power. The little ship shot out from under the *Jackson*'s belly like a minnow darting from under a shark.

The gee force was strong enough to press them back into their seats. "I don't think he'll shoot in this direction," Wilks managed to say through stretched lips. "He won't want to hit the *MacArthur*. I hope."

"I . . . hope . . . you're . . . right," Billie said.

This time, Wilks was.

The escape pod shot past the following ship so fast it was only a blur on their scopes.

# 29

Spears shook his head as he raised from his squat next to the drive housing. There weren't any bombs connected to the gyro-switch complex. Nor had there been any in the other locations. The son of a bitch had bluffed him. He felt a moment of irritation, an urge to wrap his hands around the man's throat and throttle him, but it passed. It didn't matter. So one marine and one civilian had saved their skins by lying to him. So what? After he demonstrated how he would liberate Earth, who would believe such a story, assuming that tricky bastard sergeant and his woman were foolish enough to try to spread it around? The guy was career marine, he knew what pissing off a general was worth in the long run. No, chances were they'd dig in somewhere and pretend to be invisible. If they kept quiet, there was a chance he wouldn't find them later; if they shot their mouths off, they'd leave a trail. No. It wasn't going to happen.

Of course there might be bombs hidden somewhere here on the *MacArthur* but Spears didn't believe it for a second. No, he'd been foxed. Once more, he offered a two-fingered salute to Wilks. Good marine, that one.

"Did we make it?"

In the tiny cabin of the pod, Wilks blew out a big breath. "Yeah. We did. He's outside our radar range, but he must have gone back to the cargo ship to check it out. I'd love to see his face when he realizes there weren't any explosives rigged."

"I'll pass on seeing his face again, thank you."

Wilks laughed. Then frowned. "He got away, though. He beat us and got away. I wanted to get him in my sights."

"You ought to be glad he didn't get us in his sights. Where are we, by the way? And where are we going?"

"We'll be inside Luna's orbit in another couple of days, if the guidance computer on this piece of junk can be trusted. I'm getting some signals from the region, too faint to hear much. Could be automatic from Earth. Or something from the colony on the moon, if it's still there. Gateway Station in L-5 orbit, maybe. I've got the scanner set to pick up the strongest input and home in on it. You can shuck the suit if you want. There's a chemical toilet in the back, behind the blue partition. We'll have to sleep in our seats and our diet will be a bit limited, but we should make it okay."

"You did real good back there, Wilks. You're a lot smarter than you let on."

"You think so?"

"Yeah, and a *whole* lot smarter than you look." She smiled and he returned it. He fucking hated losing Spears, but she was right. It was better to be alive to fight another day and at least they had that much.

Spears brought the queen out of deep sleep first, still securely in her cage, of course. She could see him through the clear walls, and he flicked the cigar lighter over and over, watching the little flame reflect off the heavy kleersteel plastic.

"Oh, yes, I know you remember me. The time has come for your children to go forth and do battle. You can lay a million eggs if you do as you're told, if my soldiers obey me as they should. Do you understand?"

He put his hand on the plastic.

The queen turned her head slightly, but did not move.

She understood, he was sure of it. Not the words, maybe, but she was smart enough, he knew that. The drones weren't too swift, their wattage was real dim, but the queen wasn't stupid. She knew him, and she remembered him and he was certain he'd put the fear of God in the form of Spears into her. It would all go the way it was supposed to go. And soon, the moment would be upon them.

"Approaching vessel identify yourself," the call came. "This is Gateway Station calling."

Wilks smiled at Billie. "This is the escape pod

from the Colonial Marine vessel *Jackson*," he said. "Two passengers aboard, uncontaminated, repeat, no alien contamination of this ship."

"Escape pod *Jackson*, open your control modem for grid computer override."

They were still far enough away so the transmission turnaround time took a few seconds. Wilks gave control of the pod's engines to the grid computer.

"Pod *Jackson*, you are in the grid. We'll fly you in lazy eights until the decontamination team can rendezvous your vessel. Estimate arrival time nine hours."

"Copy, Gateway. We'll be here."

Billie lifted an eyebrow.

"They have to check us out to make sure we aren't carrying any little toothy surprises," he said. "That means the station is clean. Gateway is pretty big, half the size of the old Luna One colony. Twelve, fifteen thousand people before the trouble on Earth. Probably built a few more modules since then to make room for escapees. We'll be quarantined until they are damned sure we're not infected, that'd be my guess. Run us through a CAT scanner or a fluorproj and then we're home free."

"I can't believe it," she said. "We're finally going to get somewhere safe."

Maybe, he thought. But looking at her face, he didn't say it. He only nodded.

It would take most of his remaining fuel to land the carrier, but he had the APC for his own return to orbit. The reason he had brought the *MacArthur* was that it could stand a dunking in atmosphere and normal gravity. He expected to take heavy casualties, despite the training and arms his men had, but that was to be expected, and the ship would have to stay behind. It was unimportant.

As the ship spiraled down toward its landing in South Africa, Spears showered, shaved, and put on his dress blacks. He strapped the revolvers on, the sword in its sheath, his boots. Looked at himself on the monitor. Sharp. The way a commanding general should look. Fit, ready, imperial, almost.

He took one of the remaining cigars and tucked it into his belt, to open and light when the ship achieved a landing. The troops were already being decanted, although the queen was still safely in her cage. By the time they reached the ground, they would be ready. There would certainly be a hive nearby, he had his computer searching for one, and they would put down close to it. When the wild aliens streamed out to attack the ship, they would get a big surprise.

The cameras were on, the automatic director picking the most dramatic shots according to the program Spears had installed. Low angles on him, mostly, with plenty of background stuff he could cut together later.

Fully dressed, Spears moved to the staging area where the troops, numbers glowing dimly on their heads, stood quietly, awaiting their orders. Slime dripped from their mouths and there was a slight clatter of hard chitin when they moved or touched each other.

"Stand by, men," Spears said.

He went to strap in for the final approach.

Weather radar said there was a storm front mov-

ing across the landing area. Damn. He had hoped
for a sunny afternoon. Well. The cameras could adjust for the lighting; he could clean it up when he
edited it. Besides, a little lightning and rain would
only add to the drama. This was all background
stuff anyway. Once they were down, he would have
his computers send out a live broadcast of the battle. The fortunate watchers could say they had
seen it as it actually happened.

On Gateway Station, Billie and Wilks cleaned up
and went to make their report to the powers-that-
were. A lot had happened since they'd left Earth,
nearly all of it bad. So the medic leading them to
the debriefing station said.

"Yeah," the man continued, "nobody knows how
many people are still alive downlevels. Those who
are are pretty tough and good at hiding."

Billie thought about the little girl she had seen
on the 'casts back at the military base. Was she still
alive?

"Hey, Henry, check this out."

The medic leading them slowed as a woman
nearby waved at them. "Whatcha got, Brucie?"

"Live 'cast from Earth. Look."

Billie and Wilks moved with the medic.

"Jesus," Billie said. "Spears!"

Henry and the woman Brucie turned to look at
her. "You know this nut?"

Billie and Wilks looked at each other. "Yeah,"
Wilks said. "We're old friends."

The ramp lowered and Spears walked out into
the rain. His hat brim offered enough protection so

the cigar stayed lit, though it was getting pretty damp. He sucked on it hard to keep it going.

In the rainy distance Spears saw shadowy forms approaching. He drew his sword and pointed at them. "First squad, front and center. Second squad, fan out and cover the flanks."

He had decided to hold off on giving his men weapons until he saw how his close combat tactics worked.

Number 15 moved close to Spears. Turned its head and looked at him.

"Go get them, trooper," Spears said. He waved the shining stainless-steel blade.

Number 15 stood motionless. Then its mouth gaped and jellylike drool dripped from its open jaws.

"I gave you a direct order!" Spears said.

Number 15's inner jaw oozed past the outer teeth.

"I'll not have disobedience!"

Spears swung the sword. It was heavy, made of good surgical stainless, with an edge sharp enough to shave with. The blade caught the alien's thin neck. The strike was perfect, slicing between the vertebrae into the thinner and more flexible material over the spine.

Number 15's head toppled off and fell.

Enough acid clung to Spear's sword blade so that it immediately began to smoke. The metal dissolved and ran under the pattering of the rain.

Spears stared at the ruined blade. "Goddammit!" He dropped the sword and pulled both of his S&W revolvers. He fired at the corpse of Number 15.

•   •   •

"Holy shit," Brucie said.

Wilks and Billie stared. Wilks looked down and realized that Billie was holding his hand.

Half a dozen of the troops came out of the ship behind Spears. They were carrying the queen in her cage. She made a gesture at one of them and it fumbled with the locking mechanism.

"Get away from that!" Spears yelled. He emptied the remaining rounds from his revolvers at the drone—Number 9 he saw—to no effect. The soft lead bullets flattened against the recruit's armor.

The cage door opened.

Spears dug for his cigar lighter. Held it up so the emerging queen could see it. Flicked the lighter on. Despite the wind and rain, the lighter's flame sprang up and danced in the storm.

"Fire, see! I'll burn every fucking egg you ever laid! Fire!"

"Oh, man," somebody said. Billie wasn't sure who. She was squeezing Wilks's hand hard. And he was squeezing back.

The queen paused in front of Spears, looking down from her four-meter height.

"That's right, bitch! I'm the man with the fire! I cook the babies! Fuck with me and we'll scramble some eggs, you bet!"

Like dogs, the aliens could not really smile. But the queen seemed to, the way her jaws moved. She flicked out one of her smaller arms and slapped the lighter away.

"Fuck—!"

Then she grabbed Spears and lifted him, using her larger arms. He struggled, cursed, pulled the cigar from his mouth, and tried to poke her with the glowing end. It was all going wrong! It wasn't supposed to be like this! He was supposed to be in control!

The queen reached up and caught Spears around the throat with one mighty claw.

"Don't do it, men!" he screamed. "Don't listen to her! *I* am your commander now! Obey me! Stop her! Stop her!"

Those were his last words. His last thought was that somebody had made a mistake. He had time to realize that it was him, that the queen had merely been biding her time and that her time was now—

With a quick move, the queen pulled Spears's head off. She did it as easily as a man might pull the head off a flower. She dropped the body into the mud below the ramp. Held the head for a moment longer, then tossed it aside.

As luck had it, the head hit right in front of one of the cameras, and rolled to a stop facing the lens.

The expression on the dead man's face was one of absolute horror.

"So much for the revolution," Wilks said, staring at the picture.

The onrushing aliens stopped and looked at the newcomers. After a moment the would-be attackers turned and moved off through the storm.

The newly arrived queen led her children away.

The glowing numbers on their heads were visible for quite a distance before they faded into the rain.

Quite a distance.

"Fuck," Henry said.

Oh, yeah.

# 30

After debriefing, Billie met Wilks in a conference room nobody seemed to be using. There were viewscreens on the wall, but Billie didn't feel much like looking at anything.

"He deserved it," Wilks said. "I only wish it could have been us who did it. We've been blowing around in circles for a while, kid. Haven't been much a part of the solution."

"I know."

"Then again, Spears wasn't much help, either."

Billie shook her head. "You know, crazy as he was, I was almost hoping maybe he could pull it off. I mean, I hated him, for what he was, what he did, but in a strange kind of way, I kind of wanted him to make it. Maybe I'm as crazy as he was."

"Not quite."

"Big deal. Now we're back where we were before.

The monsters rule Earth, billions of people are dead, the rest are all waiting for their turns. And there's not a goddamn thing we can do about it."

"That's a bad attitude," somebody said from the doorway.

Billie turned and looked. A woman stood there. Tall, thin, hair chopped short, wearing shipper's coveralls.

"Do we know you?" Wilks said.

"I don't think we've met before," the woman said.

But Billie recognized the face. It took a few seconds to remember where she'd seen her before. It had been back on the station, in the communications room. She'd been on one of the old 'casts.

"Ripley," Billie said. "You're Ripley."

The woman gave them a brief, small smile. "That's right."

"You're supposed to be dead," Billie said.

"From what I hear, so are you two. The universe is just full of surprises, isn't it?" She grinned again, a little larger.

"Damned if that ain't so," Wilks said.

"I think we have a few things in common," Ripley said. "Maybe we ought to sit down and talk."

It was Billie's turn to smile now. "I think maybe you're right," she said. Ripley was right, after all:

The universe was just full of surprises.

## ABOUT THE AUTHOR

STEVE PERRY was born and raised in the Deep South and has lived in Louisiana, California, Washington and Oregon. He began writing fulltime in 1978. He is the author of a number of science fiction and fantasy novels, most recently *Brother Death, Black Steel*, and the nationally bestselling *Aliens™: Book 1: Earth Hive*, as well as works for young adults and several Conan novels. He has written a number of teleplays, including those for *The Real Ghostbusters* and the new animated *Batman* television series. His short fiction has been published in magazines ranging from *Omni* to *Pulphouse*, as well as various anthologies. He has also taught classes in writing in the Portland and Washington Country public school systems, and adult writing classes at the University of Washington in Seattle. He has just finished, in collaboration with his daughter, Stephani Perry, the third novel in the *Aliens™* series, *The Female War*. Perry now lives near Portland, Oregon with his wife, who edits and publishes a small newspaper.